M000283731

SOMETHING KINDRED

SOMETHING KINDRED

CIERA BURCH

FARRAR STRAUS GIROUX
NEW YORK

Farrar Straus Giroux Books for Young Readers
An imprint of Macmillan Publishing Group, LLC
120 Broadway, New York, NY 10271 • fiercereads.com

Copyright © 2024 by Ciera Burch
All rights reserved

Library of Congress Cataloging-in-Publication Data is available.

Our books may be purchased in bulk for promotional, educational, or
business use. Please contact your local bookseller or the Macmillan
Corporate and Premium Sales Department at (800) 221-7945 ext. 5442
or by email at MacmillanSpecialMarkets@macmillan.com.

First edition, 2024
Designed by L. Whitt
Printed in the United States of America

ISBN 978-0-374-38913-0
1 3 5 7 9 10 8 6 4 2

FOR MY MOM, LAKIESHA LITTLES,
FOR ABSOLUTELY EVERYTHING.

FOR MY GRANDMOM, LUVON HENRY,
FOR DOING THE BEST YOU COULD WITH WHAT YOU HAD.

Perhaps home is not a place but simply an irrevocable condition.

—*James Baldwin*, Giovanni's Room

I feel it is the heart, not the eye, that should determine the content of the photograph.

—*Gordon Parks*

SOMETHING KINDRED

ONE

There are only two things I know about my grandmother.

One: Her name is Carol Annette.

Two: She left Mom and Uncle Miles for good on a Tuesday morning, after promising to take them to the ice cream shop when they got out of school.

That's why it makes no sense that Mom has dragged us from New Jersey, all the way to Maryland, to take care of her for the *entire* summer. Except for the fact that my grandmother has cancer. I think the idea of losing her permanently freaks Mom out more than she'd ever admit.

Death does that.

So, here we are. Standing outside Douglas Memorial Hospital with mosquitoes buzzing in our ears, skin growing sticky with sweat under the afternoon sun, Mom trying to work up the nerve to go inside.

"Mom—" I start.

The automatic doors open before I can say anything else,

and it's a relief when Uncle Miles steps through them. It's weird seeing him here. We usually meet him at rest stops the size of small towns, cramming months' worth of conversation into half an hour as he gulps down coffee.

"You good, kid?" he asks, pulling me into a hug first.

"Could be better," I mumble against his chest. He smells like dryer sheets and the cab of his truck.

He snorts and lets go, turning to Mom. She's quick to wrap him in a hug. He towers over both of us but leans down and patiently waits as she holds his face in her hands. They mostly look alike except Uncle Miles has small patches of pale skin that creep up his neck and jaw, dotting the space above his right eyebrow and curling around the shell of his left ear. But they've got the same eyes, wide and long-lashed.

When he presses his left hand into Mom's, it's white all the way to the wrist.

"You ready?" he asks.

Anxiety settles over me like a familiar second skin. The trip down was normal, the same as any other long drive. It was easy to forget the dying stranger waiting for us in a hospital bed. But now I'm nervous. I've never had grandparents before, and I've never known a person who was dying. Now they're one and the same.

I wait for Mom to answer for the both of us and look at her when she doesn't. She's let go of Uncle Miles, and her arms are curled tightly around herself now, nails digging into the skin. Her jaw's clenched. Her eyes are bright with something I don't recognize.

Still, she walks through the automatic doors when they open for her, leaving us to follow.

Mom's quiet when the old woman working the front desk addresses her by name and gives us our visitor passes. She's quiet all the way up to the third floor, the top floor in this tiny hospital. It smells like sour milk and Lysol. She's quiet until just outside room 355, when she turns to me and takes my hand.

She grips it like I'm five years old and we're crossing a busy street before she opens the door.

Loud, echoing laughter greets us.

The first glimpse I get of my grandmother is of her open-mouthed smile. She's looking away from us, toward two full-figured women in the corner wearing too much costume jewelry. When they catch sight of us, their eyes flit between Mom, Uncle Miles, and me.

"Well, I'll be damned," one says. A giant rhinestone butterfly hangs from her neck. "Welcome home, Lacey."

Mom doesn't respond, but her grip on my hand tightens painfully when my grandmother looks in our direction. The room is silent. Even the click of the door, shutting as the women slip out, is muffled.

I glance at Mom. I watch the muscles in her throat work as she swallows, and I imagine a lifetime of one-sided conversations disappearing with the motion.

In the stretching silence, I turn to look at my grandmother. I notice her shock of silvery hair first, stiff enough to make itself known as a wig. She looks so much like Uncle Miles that there's a strange recognition when I glance at her, a stutter step of surprise. She has the same tilt to her head, the same small, pointed ears and high cheekbones. And her eyes. Brown, the skin beneath them vaguely bruised-looking. They look like Uncle Miles's. Like Mom's. Like my own. A genetic family heirloom.

One of the only things she left behind with her kids when she left them.

"Lacey." She speaks first, her voice warm. The vowels in Mom's name stretch with familiarity and the hint of an accent.

"Mama." I blink at the title and how easily it sits on her tongue. Mom takes half a step forward and stops. She looks more unsure than I've ever seen her. "You look . . ." She clears her throat. "It's been a while."

"It's been a lifetime," my grandmother says. Her eyes flicker from Mom to Uncle Miles. She looks slightly surprised, like she can't believe how old they've gotten. Her hands twist themselves into the bedsheets. Maybe it's from her that Mom and I get our bad nerves, the restlessness of our hands.

The recognition of myself in this woman pushes back my anxiety and makes room for anger. Why should she get to show up in any part of me, or Mom, when she decided to make herself a stranger?

"Glad to see you've filled out. You wasn't nothing but sharp edges and scraped knees as a little girl." She laughs, and it sounds like a scoff. "Used to drive me crazy."

Silence. And then Mom's voice: "I'm not a little girl anymore."

"Of course not. But in my mind, you're always a little

girl, running around the yard covered in dirt. And Miles right behind you, chubby legs all bit up by mosquitoes."

She smiles at her children. They don't smile back.

"If this is a game of trading memories," Mom says, "you'll win. Most of ours don't have you in them."

I try not to smile. One point for Mom.

My grandmother doesn't flinch. Is she updating the mental image of that little girl in her head? Fast-forwarding through thirty years of birthdays? Her expression softens. "I'd hate to think what the ones that do must feel like."

"Speaking of new memories," Uncle Miles cuts in, gesturing to me. I will myself not to shrink as everyone's eyes follow.

The stranger in the hospital bed smiles. "You must be . . ."

"Jericka. Yup. Hi."

She looks me over, then laughs, loud. "You're almost the spitting image of what I pictured Lacey looking like all grown-up." She glances at Mom. "Well. Nearly grown." Her eyes find mine again. "Jericka, huh?"

I nod. Her stare is intense, like my answer to her not-really-a-question makes up the whole of my identity: *Jericka, huh?* I wait for her to say something else. Something meaningful? Something movie-meeting perfect? I'm the long-lost grand-daughter, after all. Shouldn't we be hugging or crying or—

"Good to meet you," she says.

She looks exhausted, like the few minutes of reunion have worn her out. Mom notices, too. She clears her throat. "Maybe we should let you get some rest. We still need to go by the house and unpack and—"

"She's getting released today," Uncle Miles reminds her.

"Not this second, though, right?" There's a sharpness to her voice that I recognize as nerves.

He shrugs. "Hour or two. Only Everett's on call today and the man works slow."

Gram nods in agreement. So does Mom. However she feels about being back, it's clear she's still at least a little in tune with this town. With its people.

"Shouldn't I call you something?" I ask, suddenly anxious to etch out a place for myself among them. "Grandma? Carol Annette?"

A thoughtful look crosses her face. "Gram would be fine," she says at last.

"Cool," I say. "Great."

Gram. I test out the word in my head. It feels too familiar, like there should be history behind it instead of all the nothing that's there.

A cough comes from next door, hacking and violent. One of the machines attached to Gram beeps. This image of her in bed, gaunt-eyed and tiny, is frustrating. I try to imagine her walking out the front door and never coming back. It's hard to hate her for the past considering her present.

But I hold on to my anger with both hands. I'm angry on Mom's behalf and angry with her for dragging me here.

"I think I'm going to grab some air," Mom says suddenly. She rubs her bad wrist—broken as a little girl and not quite right since—and heads for the door.

"I'll go with you," I say, but she shakes her head.

Then she's gone, and it's just me and Uncle Miles and the stranger that is my grandmother.

I stand awkwardly by the door, caught between wanting to run after her and waiting here. Uncle Miles shoots me a sympathetic smile.

"I'll be here awhile," he says, though he told Mom this would be quick. "Wanna grab us some coffees from downstairs before you go?"

I jump at the opportunity to get out of the room. "Yes, please." I hold my hand out for money and raise my eyebrows when he drops a five into it.

He chuckles. "Small town," he reminds me. "That'll be enough."

◊

Miraculously, there's a "café" in this hospital. It's not big, about the size of a waiting room, with a vending machine and a display table stacked high with overripe fruit. But the high-light is the small coffee counter in the corner. Slouched against it with her back toward me, a girl about my age scrolls on her phone.

"Excuse me."

Her head jerks up in surprise. She raises her eyebrows as she turns around. "First customer of the day," she says, though it's past noon. She doesn't bother putting her phone away. "Who are you?"

I blink. "Is that something you ask everyone?"

"That'd be a waste of my time since I know everyone here. But not you." She leans forward against the counter and smiles. "You're new."

There's a gap between her front teeth big enough to fit the tip of her tongue into. Her skin's a deep mahogany, and my eyes linger on her a little longer than I mean them to, piecing and re-piecing her features together. Long face. High cheekbones. A cluster of dark beauty marks on one cheek. She's pretty, I realize, in the way that some people are—without question.

I look away quickly, toward the menu. There are only a handful of choices, a few variations of coffee and hot chocolate in calligraphy that's hard to read. No iced coffee in sight.

"What do you recommend?"

"Can't go wrong with black," she says. "Plus, we've got the best coffee in town."

"Best?" My eyes find hers again. "Or only?"

Her laugh is full-bodied. "Go taste the coffee down by the gas station and you tell me."

I grimace, picturing oil in a to-go cup. "Got it. Black it is. And a hot chocolate."

I pull out Uncle Miles's five, but she waves me off and steps away to prepare the drinks. I watch her hands, bright purple fingernails gleaming against the coffeepot. "I'm Kathleen, by the way," she says. "But Kat will do."

Kat's a nice nickname. It fits her better than Kathleen seems to, somehow. The shortness of it. The punchiness.

"You got a name?" she asks when she glances over at me, eyebrows raised.

Right. Obviously. "Jericka."

"You're Miles's niece." It's a fact, not a question. When I frown, she smiles. "He has single-handedly drunk enough coffee the past couple weeks to keep us in business the rest of the year. Plus, you look like him."

A small jolt of pleasure goes through me. No one's ever said that before. There's never been anyone to compare me to but Mom.

"Besides," she adds, "the whole town's been betting on whether you and your mom would show up."

I frown. "What are you talking about?"

Kat grimaces. "My dad says I don't watch my mouth as much as I ought to. All I meant is that people always show up here again, no matter how long ago they left. That's what the old people claim, anyway. So, yeah." She shrugs, giving me an apologetic smile. "They've been betting, and I've been keeping an eye out for new folks."

"Is that what everyone does here for fun?" I ask, annoyed now. "Wait for other people to come back?"

"Or wait to die. Not a ton else to do in good ol' Coldwater." She winks at me. "But, hey, you're only visiting, right?"

TWO

"While we're down here," Mom says quietly once we're back in the car, the hospital fading in the rearview, "you should probably try and see your dad."

I turn my attention from the window and the monotony of trailers and farmhouses, their yards all overgrown and littered with toys. "What?"

"Might be nice to see him in person," she says.

We talk on the phone a few times a year, but I haven't seen him in the flesh since I was three, when he and Mom split and we moved away. I don't know much about him except what little Mom has told me and what my best friend, Leslie, and I pieced together from his social media. His account is mostly just pictures of his wife, Cora, and their two kids, Kya and Marcus. There aren't any pets or fancy vacations. Nothing to be obviously envious about.

The generic birthday cards he sends in the mail are enough

contact. They usually come a month before or after my actual birthday, like some years I'm on his mind and others I'm an afterthought.

"You didn't tell him we were coming, did you?" I need to know if I'm obligated to visit him by virtue of proximity.

Mom shakes her head, and I'm relieved but not surprised. As far as I know, the only thing they talk about is money. "Word travels fast in Coldwater, though," she says. "He'll know we're here by tomorrow."

"Then I guess he can be the one to reach out," I say, turning back to the window. There's an abandoned silo in the distance, rust-colored against an ache of sky. It's high enough up to be the tallest thing around for miles.

My phone buzzes in my lap. I'm expecting Leslie and a string of emoji-filled texts asking how it's going and if I'm okay.

But it's James. My stomach flutters as I click on his name. *Hope you made it there safe.*

The dreaded dots appear beneath the message, and I hold my breath until they fade back to nothing. I wait, but nothing else comes. The screen fades to black, and I frantically flip the phone over entirely.

I last a good thirty seconds before I flip it back over again. My fingers hover over the keyboard for a while. In the end, I send a smiling emoji. Just the default, nothing fancy. I tuck my phone into my back pocket and scoot forward until I can't feel the weight of it pressing into me and against my seat.

I won't—I *can't*—think about James right now on top of

everything else. I'm so focused on not thinking about James that I don't notice Mom turn into a dirt driveway until she mutters, "Home, sweet home."

I look up.

The house in front of us is small, yellow white, and obviously old. It sits sagging on an acre of browning grass. The side facing the road has two screen doors at each corner, but large pots of dead flowers make them inaccessible. At the end of the driveway is a shed, backed by an expanse of woods at odds with the slightly hilled land surrounding the house.

So, this is where my mom grew up. As I stare, it takes a second to realize that I'm waiting for something.

Connection.

Recognition.

Neither comes. This isn't my house.

Home for me is a tiny condo in New Jersey with a squeaky third front step and a broken screen door. It's a pine tree whose branches tap against my window in the middle of the night. It's neighbors who don't pick up after their dog and blast Taylor Swift in between screaming matches. Home, for me, is something constantly, exhaustingly new. Once or twice, sometimes three times a year, Mom changes apartments. She doesn't know how to stay still. Maybe this place is the reason why. Maybe she's still trying to outrun it.

Well, there's no outrunning it now.

Instead of air-conditioning, we're greeted by a wall of hot air when we step inside, courtesy of an open-mouthed monster of a hot-water heater.

"Jesus." Mom laughs. "I forgot about this thing."

I'm halfway to melting already, and the additional heat is making it hard to breathe. "Can't you turn it off?"

"Miles'll have to."

By the time Uncle Miles and Gram pull up, we've gotten all of our stuff for the summer inside and have the screen door propped open to help with the heat.

None of us say much once we're all together. Gram pours herself a glass of iced tea, then pours one for me when I respond to her gesturing. Mom kneels next to Uncle Miles, watching closely as he fiddles with a knob on the hot-water tank.

"Is there somewhere I can, you know, put away my stuff?" I ask, eager for some breathing room. I hung my camera around my neck so it wouldn't get misplaced or banged up while we worked, and it's growing heavier by the second.

Gram's the one who answers. "There's a door off the living room," she says. "Head up the stairs. There's a room up there."

"It was me and Miles's old room," Mom adds softly.

The living room is tiny, wood-paneled and dark, with a single curtained window behind a floral-upholstered couch. The door is easy to spot. The upstairs room is wood-paneled, too, and surprisingly large. Two twin beds are pushed up on either side of the wall, matching nightstands by their sides. The only difference between them is the color of the quilts: one pink and the other purple.

I close my eyes and try to picture Mom and Uncle Miles here. In my head, their small brown faces are scared but familiar. They're pressed close together in the pink-quilted bed with their heads tucked under the covers. It's hot and hard to breathe, but neither of them wants to poke their head out to see if the monster downstairs—yelling, breaking anything that shatters loudly enough—has decided to bring his anger upstairs to shatter new things, like bone.

In the hospital earlier, when Uncle Miles and I were waiting for Mom to come back so I could leave with her, I asked him a question that had been bugging me the whole drive down here.

"Do you forgive her?"

"Who?"

"Gram. Here she is, practically on her deathbed, and there aren't any consequences for her. You're here. Mom's here. Even I'm here. Why?"

Why should she get to be surrounded by family instead of alone somewhere, thinking about what she's done?

"I don't know if I forgive her," he said. "Or if it matters that I do. But I love her. That didn't go away just because she did."

"But how do you know that she loves you?"

"My love for her isn't based on her love for me," he said. "For me, at least, that's not how it works."

But it should be. At least for a parent. How can you love the person who is supposed to care for and protect you if they don't do either of those things? How can you love someone if they're not there?

You can't love empty space.

I open my eyes and place my camera on the purple-quilted bed.

Here, I text Leslie.

Her response, a single crying emoji, is immediate.

I stare at it longer than I mean to. At once, it takes on the weight of my entire ruined summer. This was supposed to be a big one. My last with Leslie before she went away to college. We were supposed to speed up and down the highway with the sun in our eyes, searching frantically under the seats for change at every tollbooth as we drove from beach to beach.

My head pounds. Maybe it's the heat. More likely, it's all that's to come. I climb into my new bed, shoving the heavy quilt away, and shut my eyes until the pounding stops.

THREE

"It can't be that bad," Leslie says over the phone the next morning. I'd slept through the afternoon and the night, waking to the insistent buzzing of a fly in my ear and the vibration of my phone in my pocket.

The slap of her slippers against the linoleum is audible as she walks into her kitchen, her brothers arguing in the background. I know that kitchen better than any of the ones I've called my own. Definitely better than the one behind me, the smell of bacon wafting through the screen door to find me on the porch. It's a strange sort of homesickness that I suddenly feel for a house and a family that aren't my own.

"Which part?" I ask, popping in my headphones and dropping into the kitchen chair I've dragged outside. It's hot out for so early in the morning. "The tiny town? The awkwardness in the house? The whole thing with James?"

She laughs. "All of it, including the nonexistent thing with James. You've barely been there two days. Chill."

Since the day we met in eighth-grade biology, where I had a panic attack over dissecting a frog, 90 percent of Leslie's advice has been for me to chill. It's what she said when I showed her my study schedules for the SAT, when I decided to stop straightening my hair for the first time, when I stressed over Mom's constant, pointless moves and my need to stay back a grade because of them.

"I'm trying," I say, which is a lie. It's always a lie. Even the chillest version of myself is too high-strung for her. "But I think forty-eight hours is the appropriate allotted freak-out time."

She rolls her eyes, which fill my screen. Only the top half of her head is visible thanks to wherever she's put the phone. "Fine. There's not much you can do about the whole Dying Grandma, Shitty Town thing except keep trying to convince your mom to let you come back and stay with me for the summer. Did you at least call James?"

I sigh. "No? I mean, I texted him. Do you think I should call?"

"You had sex with him for the first time and then left town for the *entire* summer. Of course you should call him. Even if it's only to break up with him."

I grimace. The problem is that I don't know *how* I feel about it. It was kind of like a goodbye or the end of a chapter while also being this monumental thing to bring us closer together.

And it had.

Sort of.

It wasn't what I'd expected. There was someone's cousin's dad's beach house and most of James's graduating class. There was beer and wine and sparklers and the entirety of the beach at night, all cool sand and gentle, lapping waves against my bare feet. We'd broken away from the rest of the party with a few blankets and, well. It just felt like the thing to do.

We drove back home the next morning. And the day after that, I was on the road heading here.

"I'm not going to break up with him," I say.

"Then call him before he gets the wrong impression." Leslie adjusts the phone to glare at me. "Or, you know, decides he likes sex enough to do it with someone else while you're gone."

"I don't know what I'm supposed to say," I admit. "Or what he wants to hear. I can't exactly tell him I think it was a bad idea when I have no clue why I feel this way."

"So, don't mention it. Play the dying-grandma card or talk about the weather. Look, I've gotta go. Robbie is about to start a food fight with all the cereal we have. But did you figure out what you're doing about the photo project yet? It's no Garden State"—Leslie's voice drips with sarcasm at the title—"but I'm sure there's something in Maryland worth taking pictures of."

Right. The photo project. For Parsons, my dream school.

I had planned to photo-document my summer in New Jersey for my portfolio, *The Hidden Beauty of the Garden State*. Now all I've got are the endless roads and fields that make up Coldwater. The occasional house. They'd make for a riveting project. *Definitely* college application worthy.

I groan. "One crisis at a time, please and thank you. Go ahead, hang up. Leave me to wilt in the Maryland sun."

She snorts. "Find something to do with yourself, drama

queen. Besides sitting in your creepy little attic room all sum-mer. Promise me."

"Well, we *are* going to go to the grocery store later . . ."

Leslie takes my sarcasm in stride. "Great! Go. Look cute. Make friends. And I mean it about getting out of the house." I open my mouth to protest—technically I *am* outside—and she glares at me. "Out of the house and *off the porch*."

I catch the quick movement of the phone as she sets it down, her voice moving farther away and going up an octave— "*Robbie*, I swear!"—before it goes dead.

"Morning," Mom greets me from her spot at the stove when I step inside. The kitchen is a messy burst of sun. It's painted a cheery yellow with pots and pans filling the sink and overflowing onto the counter. "You're up early."

I glance at the clock and shrug. "Fell asleep early."

When she glances at me, I catch the dark circles under her eyes. It must have been a long night for her surrounded by the familiar sounds of her childhood. "You planning to at least wash your face before you eat?"

"Nope." I reach for the plate of bacon she sets on the table. "It's just gonna get greasy anyway."

She shoos me into a chair and brings over another plate, piled high with scrambled eggs, before she sits, too. "Where's Gram?" I ask between bites. She's added maple syrup, and it's candied the bacon so it's perfectly chewy. If it's a peace offering for dragging me here, it's a start. "Didn't she want breakfast?"

"I didn't get the chance to ask," Mom says, turning her attention to her phone.

"Okaaaay," I say slowly, "guess it's my job, then." With half a strip of bacon in my mouth, I head through the living room to knock on the door that I guess is hers.

"Come in," she calls. Her voice is raspy. I wonder whether it's due to age or sickness or if she's just always sounded like this.

The room smells stale, but light billows in through pale blue curtains. Despite the heat, my grandmother is sitting up in bed with a heavy quilt draped over her. There's a flicker of surprise when she looks at me that quickly settles into recognition.

"Jericka."

The way she says my name makes it hard to tell whether she's happy.

"Yeah, good morning." I take the strip of bacon out of my mouth. "Mom made breakfast. Are you hungry?"

"I better give her some time to finish up first. Don't want her losing her appetite on my account."

I sigh, grateful I slept through whatever dinner must have been like last night. "Do you want me to bring you a plate?" I'm still angry at this woman, but I don't want her to starve.

A smile twists the corners of her lips. "I'd appreciate it."

Mom doesn't say anything when I start making a second plate. She only watches me with steady eyes. When I was younger, she'd break it out at friends' houses or in public. Her eyes-in-the-back-of-her-head stare that meant if I stepped a toe out of line we were going home. No questions asked. I make it out of the kitchen and back to Gram's room in time to watch her wash down a handful of pills with a glass of water.

"Here," I say, handing over the bacon and eggs. I realize a second later that I don't know if she likes either of them.

She thanks me, and I stand awkwardly by the door as she takes her first bite.

"Go eat with your mama," she says, like she's read my mind. "This isn't the first meal I've eaten alone. I don't need you keeping me company."

I open my mouth to protest, and then shut it. I linger another minute, shifting my weight until Gram meets my eyes.

"Go on," she says.

The dismissal makes me dig my heels into the ground. I don't know this woman. I don't owe her anything, not even a quiet breakfast alone. But I want to. At least, I want to know how a person goes from leaving her children behind to relying on them.

"What do you expect from us?" I ask.

She only raises her eyebrows. My hands curl into fists at my sides. If she's anything like Mom, I'll have to be more specific. "I mean, why'd you bother telling anyone that you were dying? Why didn't you just . . ." *Die* feels like a harsh way to end the sentence. "If you wanted to be alone so bad all this time, why didn't you just deal with this alone, too?"

"That's a big question first thing in the morning."

"I think you've had plenty of time to think of an answer."

For a while, we just stare each other down.

"Dying's not like everything else," she says finally. "Way I see it, it's a thing you might want other people around for."

FOUR

Downtown Coldwater, which is really just a single main street, is a series of brick and whitewashed buildings crowded together like fire hazards. Mom parks at the end of it so I can take a better look around. My hands are already fiddling with the focus of my camera as I get out of the car, my eyes going from storefront to storefront. There's a drugstore, an antique shop, half a dozen restaurants, and a bakery. A plain white church in the distance acts as the marker for the end of Main Street, and on the other side of the road is a small diner with a fading banner for a sign. Standing by the front door, a crab in a chef's hat grins at me.

Mom goes to stand next to it, laughing as she pokes its cheek. I snap a picture. "This is George's place," she says. "Before I ever thought about being a teacher, this was my first ever job. He had the greasiest burgers in town, which made them the best, or so he said." She frowns a little. "I don't even know if he's still alive."

"Who knows if anyone is alive in this ghost town," I mutter, glancing around the empty sidewalks.

I follow her farther down the street, lagging behind like I always do when a camera's in my hand. Some people have certain things they like to photograph—people, flowers, peeling stickers on the sides of street signs. I'm not nearly so niche. If I like something, I take a picture. If it makes me feel something that I want to remember, whether that's weirded-out or a new type of happy, I let my lens capture it.

Mom says I have a good eye.

I just think pictures are the way my thoughts take shape.

She's patient for the most part. She only "reallys" me when I spend too long trying to lie on my stomach to snap some birds arguing over a stale piece of a doughnut.

I cap my lens when we reach Food Lion. We're here bright and early, but the parking lot is full of cars. It seems like this is where the entire town has been hiding.

Uncle Miles offered to stay with Gram if we had things to do, and Mom jumped at the opportunity. "I wonder if they still have to wear the aprons," she says as we walk up to the grocery store.

"What?"

"I worked here, too. After the diner. We had to wear these silly bright gold aprons. To represent lions, apparently. So, we all started taking it literally—we'd growl at people behind their backs, walk down the aisles on all fours during closing." She shakes her head, but she's smiling. "We were such dorks."

I stare at her. It's like Mom's brain kept all of these memories in a vault and now that she's back, each one has come creeping out to remind her of the life she had here. To show her that this place is still hers, that she's knotted into its very fabric, even if I can't place her in it.

"C'mon," she says, stepping close enough that the doors open for her. "Let's go see."

The first woman who recognizes Mom drops her bread. Literally drops it, gasps, and rushes over to pull Mom into a hug. She's closer to Gram's age than Mom's and is all chatter and excitement, asking question after question only to interrupt with some anecdote of her own before Mom can answer. After she walks off, with a promise to drop by with pineapple upside-down cake and her photo album, Mom visibly shudders.

"Mrs. Brown," she says, like her name is explanation enough.

Everyone that comes up to us is friendly. They treat Mom like a long-lost sibling, with hugs and rehashed memories, and Mom goes along with it all. I'm included in the welcome, too. Coldwater-born, if not bred. Just a tiny thing the last time they saw me, they all say. By the time we make it to the checkout, I've been hugged by a dozen strangers and my cheeks are starting to hurt from smiling politely.

"Look," Mom whispers, nodding toward the cashier. "The aprons."

Sure enough, our cashier is wearing an apron that looks more yellow than gold with FOOD LION emblazoned across the chest. And she looks oddly familiar. Before I can get a better look, a loud, amused voice comes from behind us.

"They're an eyesore, for sure, but you should see the ones they bring out around Christmas."

Mom whips around, breaking into a smile. It's genuine this time. Her eyes even go squinty. "Gloria!"

Mom reaches out for a hug. When they're done squeezing each other tight, I get a closer look at Gloria. She's probably Mom's age, taller and thinner, with a wide, mischievous grin that reminds me of Leslie. She looks like she used to be, or still is, trouble.

"This," Mom says, and laughs, almost giddy. She's a completely different person all of a sudden. "This is your godmother, Gloria."

"It's nice—" I start before Gloria wraps me into a hug, too. She smells, almost overwhelmingly, like lemon.

"Don't gimme that stranger bullshit. You were my first baby before your mom up and whisked you away." She squeezes me again but stops short of pinching my cheeks. "It's good to see you all grown-up."

"Speaking of babies," Mom says, "where's Asia? She must be nearly as old as Jericka now."

Gloria waves a hand dismissively. "That girl's around here somewhere. Supposed to be grabbing another box of—there she is."

She nods at a girl heading toward us, head buried in her phone. Asia is almost the same height as her mom, bright yellow shorts emphasizing the length of her legs, her waist-length box braids nearly reaching them. She glances up to find us all looking at her and offers a confused smile. "Hey."

"Asia, this is Lacey, and her daughter, Jericka. Y'all are godsisters."

Asia looks as unimpressed as I feel, but she's polite about it. "Nice to meet y'all."

Our moms fall back into conversation, and I stand next to Asia while she focuses on her phone. She eventually glances up again, giving me a quick once-over. "So, do you talk, or . . . ?"

"I didn't think you were paying enough attention for it to matter."

She laughs, sliding her phone into her back pocket. "You're from out of state, right? Anywhere fun?"

I shrug. It depends on your definition of fun. "I lived in New York once, pretty close to Manhattan." More like an hour and three trains away, but, hey, it's close enough and Asia seems like the type of person who wouldn't care about the difference.

I'm mostly right. Her eyes widen, and she leans closer like she can smell New York on me. "Seriously? I've always wanted to go. Did you meet any famous people? Have you gone to Central Park?"

I start to reply—no and yes respectively—but she talks over me with her questions, and then with her stories. She starts to tell me about a guy she dated who went to school up there and invited her to a party but she—

"Hey." She cuts herself off with a thoughtful look. "You like parties?"

"I don't dislike them," I say.

Asia snorts. "Okay, well, there's this party on Friday. You

should come. I'm sure my friends would love to meet you and pick your brain about NYC." The acronym lengthens in her accent enough to be charming despite the fact that no one who lives in or near New York calls it that. "Besides, free drinks. And the more people you meet, the easier it is to deal with the boredom. Who do you know around here?"

The checkout line and the conveyor belt move forward quickly. Mom's busy talking, so I grab the basket from her and rush to put our things on the belt. "No one really," I say. "But—"

"Ouch! Hurts to know me and my free coffee didn't leave an impression."

I glance up. The first thing I see is the same wide grin I saw at the hospital's coffee counter. The second is Kat's name tag stuck to her bright yellow apron.

"Do you just work everywhere?" I blurt out.

Her grin only widens. "Beats sitting around."

"Oh, look, Kat's dragged herself in today." Asia's voice is high and mocking. Her earlier smile is gone, replaced with a glare I'm happy not to be on the other end of. "Yellow looks real good on you. Lucky, since you'll probably be wearing it for the next twenty years."

Kat's grin doesn't falter, but her eyes darken. "Sorry, Asia, some of us have to work for a living. We can't all be destined to become stay-at-home moms by twenty."

Asia scoffs. "Course you can't. Last I checked, two girls can't make a baby."

"Morris." The cashier in the next lane snaps at Kat. "Line."

Kat drags her eyes away from Asia to glance at her quickly growing line. Her hands begin moving quicker than I can follow. She doesn't look at me again until Mom's paid and she's handing me the final grocery bag. There's no grin now. Just perfect retail politeness before she turns from me to focus on the next person in line.

Asia grabs my arm, tugging me toward the exit after our moms. "Don't let ghost girl bother you. Bringing down people's mood is kinda her thing. Just ignore her."

"'Ghost girl'?" I repeat, but she ignores me.

"So, the party," she says. "Pick you up at eight?"

"Um." I glance back at Kat. She's ringing up someone else, purple nails flashing with every item she scans.

I should say something to Asia about what she said, or ask what her issues with Kat are. But we've just met. And whatever's going on between them probably isn't my business. I'm not ready to be completely friendless in this place yet.

"Yeah, sure," I agree, turning to face her again. "Eight works."

FIVE

Taking pictures is familiar. Soothing. It's the first thing I do in every new apartment—take pictures of the lobby and the elevator buttons and the view of my room from the door. It helps make those places feel a little more real when they get hard to remember after we've moved on again.

I try that with Maryland now. Just snaps of little things. Bees lazily flitting between wildflowers. The shed next to the house, white and rust-stained, and the ancient-looking wheelbarrow propped up against the side of it. I'm about to snap a picture of a pair of fat, brown-feathered birds resting on a telephone wire when my phone buzzes. It's only a text from Mom, but the vibration reminds me that I still haven't talked to James.

I take a deep breath, inhaling fresh air and summer grass, birdsong and sunlight. Then I dial his number. He answers on the third ring, just when the dread kicks in and I'm hoping he won't.

"Jericka?"

"Hey."

"Hey." I can hear the smile in his voice. "How are you? How's Maryland?"

"Fine. Y'know. Hot. The humidity is killing my hair." I cringe. I doubt Leslie meant for me to actually talk about the weather. "It's . . . weird."

"Weird how?"

"Weird like everyone knows Mom and thinks they know me by default. Weird like the past is so . . . present here."

"Maybe you're projecting," he suggests.

I stiffen. "I'm not—"

"I just mean," he continues quickly, "that maybe things are weird because they're new to you. Small towns are weird in general, you know. Everyone knows everyone else, and you've never had to deal with that before."

Of course, I have. That's basically what being the perpetual new kid means—always being on the outside of every friend group and clique. Leslie was my anchor, but it didn't help when we moved towns instead of just apartments and she was a district or two away. But I get what he means. The knowing here goes back decades. Generations.

"The mortifying ordeal of being known," I grumble, and he laughs.

"Exactly. Besides, it's only been a couple days. You'll adjust. You always do."

I smile even though he can't see me. This is how it is with

James. Comfortable. Familiar. In all my anxiety about talking to him, I'd forgotten.

We chat for a while. Until the sun doesn't feel as hot on the back of my neck as it did. Until I'm a calmer version of myself. And just when I think we're going to make it through the entire conversation without talking about our last night together, or what the future holds for us, he says:

"About the other night . . ."

I try my best not to groan. I only succeed because I know he's nervous, too. "What about it?"

"It was fun. I mean, I had fun," he stutters. "I'm glad it happened, but . . ."

My fingers tighten around the phone. "But what?"

"But it seems like you weren't glad. And I'm not really sure how to bring it up without making things awkward like I am at this very second."

"We really don't need to . . ."

"But we do need to talk about it. We need to talk about a lot, Jer. You can't just keep avoiding me."

"We had sex," I say. "That's not exactly how you avoid someone."

"You know what I mean. I feel like you only slept with me so we didn't have to talk about whether we're doing the whole long-distance thing in the fall or not. You didn't even tell me you were leaving for Maryland."

I keep quiet. He's not wrong. At least, not entirely. I'd been curious, too. I like James. I wanted to see if I'd like him more, after. But I'm still not sure.

He sighs. "Should I take this whole thing as some kind of hint? Because if you want to break up with me, I won't stop you. But I'm not going to do it for you, either."

I tilt my head back until all I can see is sky. "That's not what I want," I whisper to James and the clouds.

"Then what do you want?"

I want to find a good theme for my portfolio. I want to get into Parsons. I want to live somewhere for longer than a year and really get to know my neighbors. I want to call somewhere home instead of a Frankenstein mash-up of all the apartments I've ever lived in.

The problem is that none of those things involve James. Not really.

"I just want time to think, okay? There's so much going on right now that I just . . ." Need space. "Need time to process everything."

We're running out of time for thinking. He goes to DC in August, off to college and new opportunities, and I know he wants things solidified before then, if only for peace of mind. But I can't give him that right now. Not when peace and surety are the furthest things from my own mind.

"Everything feels a little up in the air right now with Gram being sick, you know? Like some things can sit on the back burner for a bit."

"Sure," he says finally, after a pause long enough that I think he's hung up. "Of course. I understand. I'll still be here while you process."

He will be. Because he's always there, somehow so sure

about me in a way that I can't seem to fathom, let alone return. I wish I could ask him how he does it. But asking would probably be admitting that I can't picture our relationship in the same way that he does. And that isn't fair to do when I don't know whether my fear of the future is James-specific or just an all-encompassing fear of everything yet to come.

SIX

I stay outside with my thoughts until the heat drives me back in. It's only after I've been in the living room for a few minutes, sitting in the armchair closest to the fan, that I realize Gram is here, too. She's on the couch watching something black and white and grainy on TV.

"What are you watching?" I ask. I can do this. I can sit in the living room and try to talk to my grandmother about something other than her abandonment.

"*The Duke Is Tops.* 1938. Lena Horne."

I turn back to the TV with renewed interest. "I know this one," I say. "Her boyfriend's some kind of traveling salesman, right?"

Gram nods, glancing over at me. She looks a little impressed. "You know old films?"

"They're a hobby of mine," I admit. Between photography and old movies, I might as well be seventy, not seventeen, or so Leslie likes to tease. "Mom got me into some of them, and I found the rest on my own."

"Got a favorite?"

"*In the Heat of the Night.* Definitely. Have you *seen* young Sidney Poitier?"

She laughs. "Course I have." Her smile goes soft around the edges, but she keeps her eyes on the TV. "Glad Lacey kept up the tradition."

"What tradition?"

"About once a month, when Charlie was working late, me and the kids would get together down here. I'd let them pick an old tape to watch. Sometimes we'd make popcorn, even though the smell lingered and we'd have to open every window in the house to get it out before their dad got home."

There's something sad about the memory despite how happy it sounds—something trapped and stifling. I'm only half watching Lena Horne sing, when my phone buzzes. It's Leslie, responding to a text I sent after talking to James. I scan the preview of it, a half dozen emojis from surprise to despair, before flipping the phone over. I don't want to talk about this now. I'm having enough trouble trying not to think about it.

I should go look for Mom so we can talk. That's what I'd usually do. But I'm still upset about her dragging me here. Besides, she likes James, and I need someone unbiased. Someone who doesn't know either of us.

I glance at Gram. "Can I ask you something?"

She makes a noise that sounds like either a yes or a

half-asleep murmur. I ask anyway. "How do you know if you love someone?"

Gram sits up and looks at me, more alert now, like there's some trick to my words. "You ask yourself if you love 'em. If the answer's no, or you have to think too hard about it, you probably don't."

It's not that simple. James is one of my best friends. He makes me laugh and he knows what to say to cheer me up. He knows my Starbucks order and remembers how much I hate mushrooms. Being with him is as comfortable as being alone, even when I'm drained. I like him. I *really* like him.

"I could probably love James if I had more time," I say aloud.

My grandmother snorts. "You're young, there are other people to love. What's the point waiting around for it to strike?"

I sigh. "It would make everything easier."

"Listen," Gram says. "Nobody in the history of the entire goddamn world has ever had anything completely figured out. Why should you be the first? Why would you want to be?"

Because it would probably save me a lot of time spent worrying. I shrug and she shakes her head at me.

"All the fun's out there, in that future you're so scared of."

"All the scary stuff, too," I point out.

"Like what?"

"Like failure."

This is supposed to be the most important time of my life. I'm prepping for senior year and college and the new me that's supposed to manifest there. It's like I'm anticipating this strange human metamorphosis without the comfort and privacy of a cocoon.

Gram purses her lips from side to side like she's rolling a mint in her mouth. "You're gonna fail. Sometimes it'll be big. Sometimes you won't be able to fix it. You can't go through life winning everything. Now, about this James boy," she says once my quiet has settled into a worried, buzzing thing. "Lemme see him."

I hesitate, but take out my phone anyway. I watch as she looks him over. Tall, sweet James with skin like soil—rich and warm. His curly hair is cut low and he has a perfect post-braces smile. He'd still had them on when we met.

"I had sex with him," I say, and immediately realize that's not the kind of thing you should say to your grandmother. When I peek at her, though, she only laughs. It makes her look like Mom.

"Well," she says, drawing out the word, "good for you. Still don't mean you love him." She hands the phone back. James smiles up at me from the screen before it fades to black. "I wouldn't worry about it. It's rare when love makes anything easier."

I snort. She says it like worrying isn't basically a hobby for me at this point. Not that she would know. We're strangers sharing a house, my grandmother and me. For a second, it was almost easy to forget.

"Did it make leaving easier?"

I don't mean to ask, at least not out loud. But it's hard to think of anything else in her presence.

"Not the leaving, no. But the staying gone, sure."

Half an hour later, the movie ends, and Gram says, "Help me with something a minute."

In her bedroom, she riffles through the top drawer of a dresser. It's scratched, fading brown, and its gold handles are either loose or missing completely. She yanks at them with increasing frustration, working her way down, as I stand in the doorway watching her.

"Damn thing," she grumbles as a drawer gets off track. The bottom busts and a box tumbles out, an avalanche of photos and papers following. I kneel to help, and even as she shoos me away, she accepts the pile I scoop up. "Put everything on the bed."

I do. Crumpled papers covered in scribbled cursive sit next to birth certificates and sepia-colored photos and faded crayon drawings. It's my family's history, scattered on the bed. Gram perches on the edge and becomes part of it.

"I took all this with me when I left. The kids' drawings and our pictures, too." She strokes the edge of a faded photo with veiny hands. They're small, but not too wrinkled. She's not as old as I keep imagining her to be. Not quite old enough to die. "Memories of loving and being loved, I guess."

She looks incredibly young in one of the pictures. Barely older than I am. She's standing in a long floral dress, with perfectly pressed and curled hair, next to a tall, bearded man who I assume is my grandfather. Both of them are wearing wide smiles. A toddler version of Mom clings to her leg. A chubby baby version of Uncle Miles wails in her arms.

"I was fifteen when we met. Seventeen when we got married. Not even twenty when I had Lacey. Charlie was my world for a long time, and he was a good one, before the drinking. I loved him, and you're willing to overlook a lot when you love someone. S'almost scary how much you cling to everything that came before all the bad."

"So, what happened?" I ask, picking up a piece of paper closest to me. It's a drawing. A triangular sun is shoved into a corner and the grass is a squiggly green line. In the sunless top right corner is a signature; I can just barely make out the *L* at the beginning. Mom drew this. "What made you finally leave?"

"Wasn't one thing. Things had been bad and I was getting antsy, you know? Like how a body gets when you've been somewhere awhile and you just want to get home. That's how I felt, except there wasn't no going home. I was already there. But I had plans. Ideas. Little by little, I started squirreling stuff away. Kept it down the road at Sheila's, since she was the closest." She laughs and it's dry as a cough. "Stupidest thing I could've done. Nosiest woman in the state, that one, and she sure enough mentioned it to her husband. He was drinking buddies with Charlie.

"Well, soon as he got word I was moving stuff around, he didn't even bother hitting me. Just kept watch like a hawk. Only time he didn't was when the kids were at school, 'cause he knew I wouldn't go anywhere without them. Well." She snorts. "I showed him. I left, and I promised myself I'd go back for them before the week was out. Then the month. Then the school year. By the time their birthdays came around, I couldn't bring myself to step foot back into this town. I was too scared I'd get stuck again. I was more scared of that than the idea of my babies growing up without me, to tell you the truth."

Gram clears her throat. I can hear how close her tears are to the surface. "That doesn't make up for after he was dead and buried, of course. That was all me. But they had a good life with their grandmother, and I didn't see the point in messing that up for them."

"You could have given them the choice." I've heard of Grandma Jean and how much Mom and Uncle Miles loved her. How much better things were for them with her than they had been in a while. Maybe ever. But even so.

She shrugs. "No point in 'could haves.' It's past." She starts to gather everything spread out on the bed, eager to return history to the small box.

"Wait," I say quickly, placing a hand over the pile. "Can I look at these for a minute? I'll put everything back."

She holds my gaze before she nods. "It's your history, too, I guess." She stands, and even though the movement looks pained, she doesn't let it show on her face. She's nearly out the door before I call to her. "Gram?"

"What?"

"Thanks."

I pick up the family photo first. When I was little, I was convinced every picture in the world had me in it because every photo in our house had me in it. It's hard to pinpoint when I realized that wasn't the case. That most people had family, sometimes even huge, extended ones, and pictures with them.

I had Mom and occasionally Uncle Miles. They were enough except for when they weren't.

I caught Mom off guard one day when I asked why we didn't have any family. She put down the mail she was holding to frown at me. "What do you mean?" she asked.

I didn't know what I meant. Not really. Mostly, I wanted to know why I had no grandparents' house to sleep over at. Why I had no cousins to play with. Why, as much as I loved her and I knew she loved me, it felt a little bit lonely with just the two of us.

"Why's it just us?" I was frustrated. Mom was my whole world, but she'd had to come from somewhere. From someone.

When you're a kid, it's hard to understand that your parents are people. They have actual names and parts of their lives that exist without you. So, when Mom started to cry, like a person instead of a mom, I didn't know what to do. She didn't cry very hard or for very long, but her tears shocked me.

I touched her cheek, brushing away her tears the way she always did mine. "Don't cry."

When she pulled me into a hug, her tears dripped onto my hair and down my face until it felt like I was crying, too. "I'm sorry," she apologized. "I'm sorry."

We didn't sit like that for long. Mom's always been good at not wallowing in her own sadness.

It's easy to see that version of Mom in the wallet-size picture in my hands. She's a baby, all wide eyes and springy curls, and she's curled on someone's lap. I can't tell who the person is, but Mom seems content. She stares into the camera, or at the person behind it, with a gummy little smile.

SEVEN

There's only one bathroom in the house, and Mom comes in while I'm doing my hair Friday night. She smiles at me in the mirror, all soft, like I'm getting ready for prom instead of a house party.

"Want some help?"

"I guess." We haven't talked much about, well, anything. But my hair is still a mystery to me after seventeen years and I'm not about to turn down her help.

She sits on the toilet lid, and when I sit on the floor, between her legs, I'm nine years old again. Mom's hands are in my hair, yanking and braiding with familiar motions. All that's missing now is a plastic container full of ballies and barrettes and a bottle of pink lotion.

Besides the quick slaps to my shoulders to make me stop squirming and the forceful turns of my head, mornings before school were my favorite. Unlike the evenings, when Mom was exhausted from grading papers and I was swamped with homework, mornings were when we got to talk. I talked about everything—who'd gotten in trouble the day before, what new things I'd learned, the latest bus gossip—and Mom listened. She remembered the names of briefly mentioned classmates and who said what weeks ago. Sometimes she talked, too, and I did my best to listen as well as she listened to me.

But then the moves got to be too much. I stopped learning people's names and it got harder to keep track of who was friends with whom, especially when no one was friends with me. I stopped seeing much of a point in telling her about what was going on. After fourth grade, it just didn't seem worth it.

"I know this move was hard," she says finally. "I know it's the farthest I've brought you, and I know you had plans. And I am sorry about that." I startle. Mom never apologizes, at least not out loud. "But it's hard for me, too. Especially when I promised myself I wouldn't come back."

She meets my gaze in the mirror. There's an uncertain twist to her lips and anxiety in her eyes. It makes her look younger. Vulnerable. "In a town like this, no one wants you to leave. No one expects you to. You stay, like your parents did, and your grandparents. Why would anyone leave their home? 'Home's home,'" she says, tone mocking and pitched deep like she's parroting someone. "'Good or bad.'"

Everyone comes back sometime, Kat had said at the hospital. Everyone.

I wonder what it's like to have someplace to leave.

"So, why come back? You didn't have to. Gram wouldn't

have—*couldn't* have—expected it of you. And Uncle Miles could've hired someone to take care of her."

She shoots me a look. "Help is expensive. And if Miles was going to throw himself into this, I wasn't going to let him do it alone. I'm his big sister. It's my job to be there for him."

He's an adult. An adult who drives a giant truck for a living. He probably doesn't need the help she thinks he does.

"And that's all?" I ask.

She goes quiet, smoothing down the section of hair she'd been braiding before moving on to another. "I think that's enough. But it's not all. I . . . I couldn't let her leave me again without some kind of goodbye. I'm owed that much." Her hands start up again, quicker than before, yanking tighter. "I know this is a different type of leaving, but I want her to look us in the eye this time. She doesn't get to leave consequence-free twice."

"So . . ." Why couldn't I have stayed at Leslie's and lived out my summer like I'd planned? Stuffing my face full of her abuela's chilaquiles and tanning at the beach? "What next? Is it back to the same place? Same school?" There's no same apartment, that I already know. Our lease was up; we came here instead of renewing it.

"One day at a time, Jer. I know you want to know everything. But we just got here. Let's stay awhile longer before we decide where to go next, huh?"

I scoff. "Sure."

That's the thing that drives me crazy. She plays everything

by ear without thinking of the future until it's standing right in front of us.

We sit in silence as she wraps my newly braided hair into a thick double crown around my head. Finally, she asks, "Are you excited for this party?"

Not really. But I'm excited to get out of the house. "I guess. Any Coldwater house party tips?"

"You'll be fine. House parties are pretty standard; I met your dad at one."

I turn to look at her and she repositions my head. "I thought you knew Dad since you were toddlers."

"Sure. But high school is different. You meet people for the first time all over again. You'll also . . ." She trails off, probably remembering that, besides Leslie, I'm several school districts removed from the friends I had in childhood. "Anyway. Don't be nervous because you don't know anyone. No one really knows anyone else, especially at a party."

I roll my eyes. "You're such a mom."

Chuckling, she presses a kiss to the top of my head and lets me stand to get a better look in the mirror. I look cute. I could use some makeup, maybe some highlighter, but it's too hot to think about putting anything on my face.

"Thanks," I say, offering up a smile.

Before she can respond, there's a knock at the front door. It starts off quiet and gets louder, like the knocker second-guessed whether it could be heard. It continues as I leave the bathroom and head through the living room and kitchen. I didn't expect Asia to be the type to knock instead of sending a text.

And I'm right. It's not her.

Instead, a man I haven't seen since I was a child blinks at me from behind the screen door. I blink back. Dad looms larger than I expected him to. Despite the pictures, it's strange to imagine him as more than a name squished into the left-hand corner of an envelope. Hard to think of him as an actual person living little more than three hours away.

"Jericka?"

His voice is warm and my name takes on a cadence that's at once new and nigglingly familiar. I don't know what to say, so I just stare. His head is shaved, but he has a graying beard and his eyes are hidden behind dark sunglasses. In their lenses, I can see my reflection. I reach for something to ground me and settle on basic manners. *Let him in, Jericka.*

I take a few steps back and open the screen door. He steps across the threshold, Timbs heavy enough to rattle the doorframe.

"Jericka?" Mom calls. "Who is it?"

She steps into the kitchen and freezes. "Gerard. What are you doing here?"

"Heard you were in town." The way he says it makes it clear he didn't hear it from her.

"I got a phone. You could've called before you came all the way here."

"Didn't want to give you the chance to say no."

They stare at one another and I glance back and forth

between them. This is the first time I've ever seen them in the same room. It's disorienting. I wonder if I should hug him and think better of it.

Their eyes flicker to me at the same time and I try for a smile. "It's good to meet you. See you, I guess, since we've met before obviously."

I could go on rambling polite nonsense forever, but he interrupts me with a tight hug before I do. I breathe in the scent of him—aftershave and sweat. *He gives good hugs*, I think. And then it's over, and he's staring at me like I'm some new breed of teenage girl.

"You look . . . ," he begins, and shakes his head. "You look so much like your mom at that age."

Dad clears his throat, but the look of searching awe doesn't leave him. "I came to ask if you wanted to come by for dinner. The kids and Cora are dying to see you, and I figured it'd be nice to spend some time together. If you want."

"I can't."

Dad's hopeful smile dims. I rush to replace it, to be the daughter he's built up in his head. She probably doesn't hold grudges or ask questions about where he's been for most of her life. Whoever she is, I can probably be her for one dinner.

A flash of irritation goes through me at how eager I am for his approval.

"I'm about to go to a party." As in, I can see Asia's headlights at the end of the driveway.

He blinks. "A party?"

"Ran into Gloria at the market and she had Asia invite

Jericka out." Mom steps in. Is it me or is that relief in her voice?

"But I can come another day," I add.

He smiles again in full force. "Sure. Sure, whenever you want."

"Monday?"

He looks like he's going to reach out and hug me again, but instead he just nods, stuffing both hands into his pockets. "Monday's perfect."

I head outside, watching Dad get into his car and drive away.

Then Asia beeps her horn. Loudly.

EIGHT

I take a deep breath before sliding into the passenger seat. "Hey. Thanks for the ride. And the invite."

"Yeah, no problem." She glances up from her phone and grins. "And if I hadn't invited you, Mama probably would've made me anyway." She tosses me her phone so she can put both hands on the wheel. "Text Liyah back for me, yeah?"

I fumble to catch it and spend the next ten minutes texting whatever she asks to whoever she says. It's a simple job, one I prefer to the silence that creeps in whenever she's done dictating. Outside blurs by in a pattern—forest, field, house, repeat—as she speeds down empty roads.

We pull up to a double-wide trailer. A handful of girls are sitting on the porch with drinks in their hands. Most are wearing shorts and tank tops though the night is starting to cool. The looks they give me fall somewhere between vague suspicion and curiosity. A few of them hop up with squeals that echo as we get closer and Asia hugs them before turning back to me.

"Jericka, this is Liyah, Keisha, Etta, and Frankie. The boys, Sol and Bennie, are probably somewhere inside. Girls, this is Jericka. She's from *New York*."

Close enough. It captures their attention, anyway, and all four of them turn to me with wide eyes.

"Have you met Jay-Z?"

"Have you been to the top of the Empire State Building?"

"Does it really never sleep? Like, is everything open all day, every day?"

"Uh, no, no, and kinda?" If this is what I have to look forward to for the entire party, I'm ready to go home.

"Okay, but have you ever—"

"Can we do this inside?" A girl with a halo of tight curls, who I think is Frankie, interrupts. "My song is on!"

Inside, the air is sticky. It smells of too many people crammed into too tight a space. The music is a whirlpool of late '90s, early 2000s jams remixed with something bass heavy. The samples are recognizable, and so is the tempo, but it's hurried, sped up, repetitive: a shittier version of Jersey club music.

Couples are grinding everywhere, and the entire party reminds me of a middle school dance. It's hard to move but harder to stand still. I squeeze myself into a spot in the corner and try to catch my breath. It's too loud to talk, but I call out for Asia anyway when we get separated. By the time I spot her and her friends, they're halfway across the room. She's talking to a guy—Sol, or is it Bennie?—who's leaning against a wall. He's had a shape up recently, and even from where I'm standing, the waves in his dark hair are visible. She grabs his hand and the two of them disappear into the kitchen. I catch Frankie nearby, dancing her heart out.

I take a deep, centering breath, but it doesn't help. The crowd is starting to feel like a swarm of insects. How many people can fit in this trailer? Isn't this a fire hazard? I imagine the dance floor ablaze, screams joining the club remixes as people dance away from the flames, the walls of the trailer curling in on themselves, trapping us as the place fills with smoke . . .

I shake my head. Everything is fine. I'm fine.

I dig my nails into my palms to reassure myself and spot a friendly face across the room: the snack table. Edging my way over along the wall, I reach the safe haven of food with no incidents. It's covered with trays of broken pretzels, barbecue chips, and small bowls of M&M's. No one else lingers nearby. This is for me, then, and me alone.

Yep, I think, popping a pretzel into my mouth. As long as the trailer remains fire-free and the snacks hold out, this will be no problem. By the time I decide I should start looking for Asia and her friends again, half the tray of pretzels is gone.

"Are you gonna eat all the snacks, or will you save some for everybody else?"

It's Kat.

Again.

She seems to be everywhere. But here, she looks different. For one, she's not wearing an apron. There are gold rings woven into her braids, and her eyeliner is winged and thick. A tiny gold stud glitters in her right nostril, and an amused smile lingers on her lips. There's a pretzel halfway between mine, and I chew it as quickly as possible.

"I'm probably gonna eat them," I admit. "No one else seems to be. Besides, the snacks are the best part of this party."

She laughs and pops a chip into her mouth, grinning around it. The lipstick she's wearing is a deep purple. It suits her. She looks like she belongs here. Even her eyes look brighter. They're a deep, molten chocolate. Eyes that hold the weight of her attention. Eyes currently fixed fully on me.

I wipe my hand quickly across my mouth, too aware of the crumbs probably sticking to my lip gloss.

"Not a party person, I take it?" she asks.

"I don't know anyone. And it's crazy hot and crazy crowded. I could probably get drunk if I just stand here long enough."

She glances around with the same grin—I'm starting to think *amused* is her default—and nods. "I don't think any of that matters when you're drunk. That's the point of parties like this."

"I'm not drunk," I point out. "And neither are you. So, this party just sucks."

Kat shrugs. "It's in poor taste to get drunk when you're the host."

"The . . . host . . . ?"

Of course she's the host. I start to stammer an apology, but she doesn't even look upset; she's laughing.

"Why are you laughing?" My face is flaming and my mouth is dry, partially from the pretzels. "Aren't you mad?"

"Mad about what? Everything you said is true."

"But—"

"It's a house party, Jericka," she says, and I'm weirdly flattered that she remembers my name. "I'm just giving the people what they want." She tilts her head as she looks at me and a braid falls into her face. She tucks it behind her ear. "Well, I guess, not you."

She's going to kick me out for being rude, and I'll deserve it. Even though I'd rather be anywhere but here—at this party, in this state—the thought of being kicked out in front of so many people is mortifying enough to make my stomach ache.

"Guess not," I say. I'm not altogether positive I haven't whispered it.

"C'mon, then," she says, and starts to make her way through the crowd. I stare after her, unmoving. "'C'mon, then' usually means 'follow me,'" she says, and grabs my hand. Her palm is slightly damp but soft. Her fingers grip mine tightly.

Kat navigates the mass of people easily, shaking her hips and bobbing her head in a way that people with rhythm take for granted. I follow stiffly, trying not to press too closely against her or focus too hard on the languid way her body pushes past everyone else's. We pass the doorway to the kitchen, where the smell of tequila and vomit mix, strong enough to make me gag. Then we're outside, surrounded by blessedly fresh air.

And she lets go of my hand.

NINE

The area behind Kat's house is colorful in a way that the rest of town isn't. There are vibrant shrubs studded with pale pink blossoms and even a small vegetable garden, where leafy greens and the tiny red bulbs of tomatoes are visible. Beyond that are the woods. The shadows of trees brush the sky, itself a freckling of stars, each brighter than the next. If this were a painting, everything would smudge.

"It's beautiful out," I say.

"Coldwater is on its best behavior at night. And cooler, thank God."

The heaviness of the sun is gone and there's a slight breeze now, just enough to cut through the humidity. Kat starts walking quickly and with no destination in mind that I can tell. I half jog to keep up.

"About the grocery store," I say, because the whole interaction has been playing on a loop in my head since I saw her. "I'm sorry I didn't say anything."

She glances at me. "What would you have said? 'Be nice'? You don't know either of us, and you only would have ended up pissing Asia off." She smirks at me. "Then how else would you have gotten a ride here?"

I blink. She knows I came with Asia? "You don't like her."

"Right."

"Then why are you letting her party at your house?"

"Same reason I go to the parties at her house. Coldwater's small. If you avoid the parties of everyone you dislike, all you'll be is bored at home."

Makes sense, I guess. "But she was so rude. She—"

"Implied that I was a lesbian?" Kat snorts. "Considering it's the truth, I don't really care what she has to say. If a half-hearted insult at the grocery store is the best Asia's got, I'll be fine."

"You have an answer for everything, don't you?"

She laughs. "Wouldn't be much of a conversation if I didn't."

We walk alongside the trees for a while. They're frightening in the dark. I step a little closer to Kat, and if she notices she doesn't say anything. Not about that, anyway.

"See those flashes of light over there?" She points toward a small tree standing like a guard between her property and the tree line. I nod. "It's our bottle tree."

I squint. I can just make out the branching shape of a tree—covered in what I assume are glass bottles. "Why?"

Kat shrugs. "Keeps the spirits out, and all."

Her words make me pause. She says them so casually,

like it's a tried-and-true fact and not superstitious nonsense. It reminds me of something else Asia said at the grocery store. What she'd called Kat. Ghost girl.

"Spirits?" I repeat.

"You know, ghosts? Phantoms? The lingering remains of someone's eternal soul?" Her voice is dry as if she's teasing me, but her eyes are bright. "Echoes."

I raise my eyebrows. "I don't know that last one."

She shrugs. "It's not different from the others. It's just what I call the ones that live in Coldwater."

"The ones that *live* . . . ?" I can't help the laugh that bubbles up and spills past my lips. "You think this place is haunted." It's boring, sure. And just big enough that the few people who live here make it feel empty. But *haunted*?

Kat slows to a stop and looks at me. "I don't think it. I'm telling you it is."

For a person trying to convince me that ghosts—sorry, *echoes*—are real, she doesn't look bananas.

I glance away, trying to focus on what she's saying, when it clicks. "Ha, ha. Is this some new-kid ritual? Bring the new girl out here in the dark and try to scare her with ghost stories?" I roll my eyes. "This might've worked better if you had a bonfire. Oh, or maybe you could"—I lower my voice to a whisper—"tell me an old story about whatever's lurking in these woods."

I drop the whisper, eyes darting toward the woods, thinking maybe some kids from the party will jump out to scare me. "You can come out now!"

The woods are silent. The trees don't even rustle. I frown.

"C'mon," I call again. "Show yourse—"

Kat's hand darts out to cover my mouth before I can finish. It's a warm, insistent pressure even though her fingertips are cold enough against my skin to make me shiver. We stay like that for a breath. She levels a frightened look at me and slowly removes her hand.

She glances first over my shoulder and then back over hers. I catch the quick movements of her eyes as she searches for something in the dark and note the way she relaxes when she finds nothing.

I glare at her, blotting my lips experimentally. My lip gloss is gone, probably smeared all over her palm. "What the hell was that for?"

Kat raises her eyebrows like I should be the one apologizing. "Don't you know better than to go calling for things at night?"

"I wasn't calling for anything except whoever's out there *hiding*—"

"You can't just say any old thing out here without something hearing you and deciding it's welcome."

I snort. "You mean ghosts. Echoes."

She nods.

"You're the one who brought up bottle trees and spirits in the first place."

"Yeah," she says, "because I was warning you." She frowns at me, then leans forward. She's close enough that we could share the same breath. "Didn't your mama ever tell you about them?"

"About the echoes that don't exist?" I cross my arms over my chest. "No. She didn't."

Kat chews her bottom lip as if she's trying to decide something. Whether to trust me, maybe. Or if she should keep this prank going, probably. Except she looks oddly serious.

"You know how places are known for things," she says finally. "Some historical event or a giant ball of string or a weird cult or something?" I nod. "Well, Coldwater's got its echoes. Them, and the Coldwater chill."

"The what?"

She sighs. "It's not a what. More like a feeling."

"A feeling of . . . ?"

This is silly. The more I buy into this, the more annoying it'll be when it all turns out to be a prank. But Kat doesn't look like she's about to prank me.

"I don't know if it's the same for everyone. I don't think it is, really. Most people just get the chill. That quick bite of cold in your bones, like a breeze that comes from nowhere. There and gone."

Most people, she said. "And what about for other people?"

She glances at me. "Emotion so deep it roots you to the spot. Just makes you freeze up. And it's not as random as it sounds. It's how you've already been feeling. Just stronger. Sharper. Like you walked into a room full of speakers and your own voice is the only thing coming out of each of 'em. Like a million echoes of that voice in your head telling you how awful you are. It's miserable."

Kat's voice is soft and thin, and if the wind blows a little harder, it'll be whisked away like she never spoke at all. But as quick as I hear it, it's gone. She grins, all disarming charm, and her voice is back to normal when she suddenly asks me the most random question.

TEN

"It's cancer, right?"

I blink. "What?"

"Your grandmother. She has cancer, doesn't she?"

What does that have to do with anything? Still, it's better than talking ghosts or being pranked.

I sigh. "Yeah, cancer." Though no one has bothered to even really tell me what kind or what stage. "How do you know?"

"If you're here long enough, you'll realize that the answer to that question is 'small town' every time. Everyone's curious."

"Everyone's nosy," I correct.

"Same thing. How's she doing? Miles was in all the time at the beginning, but it's slowed down some. And now you and your mom are here. Hard to tell if that's a good thing or not."

"She seems okay, I guess." I don't want to talk about this. "How's *your* grandmother?"

Kat laughs. "She's pretty dead."

"Oh."

"So, assuming you don't want to talk about dead and dying grandmothers, what do you want to talk about?"

I shrug. "I didn't expect to talk to anyone tonight." It's not a lie. I'd decided to spend all night at that snack table.

"You went to a party," she says slowly, "and didn't expect to talk to anyone at all?"

"No. Not unless they spoke to me first. I mean . . ." I huff out a breath. "I figured no one would notice me. I definitely didn't think I'd talk to you."

"Ouch. Grocery store convo drove you away, huh?"

"No! I didn't mean it like that. I just . . . I didn't expect you to be here."

"Everyone's here."

"Yeah, I can see that now. I'm not used to that at home, everyone showing up at one party."

"Home, which is where?"

"New Jersey."

She makes a vaguely interested noise. A typical response to my home state. "Not New York, then. You're gonna let down your little fan club inside."

I roll my eyes. "I think I did the second I admitted I've never seen Beyoncé and Jay-Z. What about your family?" I ask.

"What about them? Have we ever seen Beyoncé and Jay-Z? Unless they're chilling at the Food Lion or at church, that's gonna be a hell no."

"Don't they mind you throwing a party?" I elaborate. I can't imagine tomorrow's cleanup.

"The Waynes are working late. They don't ask questions.

As long as everyone's gone when they get back, they don't care."

"The Waynes?"

"Dwayne Sr. and Jr. My dad and my brother."

"What about your mom?"

"She doesn't exactly care what I do. Kinda hard to from seven hundred miles away."

The amusement in Kat's voice fades. I'm wary of this girl who talks about ghosts with reverence and moms with revilement. Fascinated, too. It's quiet for a moment, or as quiet as it can be so close to a party. Some new remix carries itself on the wind. The grass sways, dancing. I keep an eye out for ghosts and drunk people.

She shoves her hands into the pockets of her romper. "I didn't mean to get weird. I'm used to everyone here knowing enough of my business that they don't bother asking."

"I didn't mean to—"

She waves me off. "My mom skipped out on us when I was six. It was big news in town for a while, and then someone else screwed up and everyone focused on that instead."

I think of Mom and Gram, of Kat and her mom. I try to imagine what kind of town this must be to force mothers away from their daughters.

I can feel Kat's eyes on me as she waits for my response. But when I open my mouth to give it, she shakes her head.

"We've already covered echoes, let's save the childhood trauma for my next party." She lowers herself to the ground and sits cross-legged in the grass before I can blink. "So," she says, grinning up at me, "tell me about yourself."

"Is this therapy now?" I take a seat beside her. It smells like rain, past or future, and the ground is cool. I try not to think of the bugs crawling around in the dark or of all the uncomfortable twists and turns our conversation keeps taking.

Laughing, Kat unfolds herself, leaning back. I catch the gleam of her teeth in the moonlight, the wide shape of her mouth. "If it is, I wanna go first. I've got a shit ton to get off my chest."

"I'll listen for twenty bucks an hour."

She snorts. "That's robbery."

"Have you been to therapy? That's a steal."

"I couldn't talk to you anyway," she says. "I'd get distracted."

I pull my lower lip between my teeth, waiting for her to say more. Kat doesn't elaborate. I've never just sat outside in the dark, completely quiet and still, but Kat seems at home.

When I can't stand the silence anymore, I scramble for yet another new topic of conversation. "Are you going to school in the fall?" I don't even know if she's graduated, but she can correct me if she wants.

"Maybe."

I frown. "Maybe?"

"I'm going to Hampton." Her voice sounds a little smaller. Uncertain. "If I get off the wait-list."

"Didn't you apply to any other schools?" There are a million schools with a million different photography programs, but it was easy to fall in love with Parsons. Still, even after I did, I looked for others to apply to. A dozen applications to schools with amazing programs are currently sitting in a folder on my laptop, nearly finished. Contingency plans on top of contingency plans.

The moon breaks free from the clouds, and I catch Kat shrug. "Sure. But Hampton's it for me."

Graduations are over and dorm shopping season is in. I must have gone to a million different Targets with James and his mom looking for the perfect dorm decor while Kat is still waiting to hear back from her school at all.

"What if you don't get off the wait-list? If you haven't accepted any other offers by now, you might not—"

"I might not get out of here. I might not go anywhere. I know."

"If you want to leave, why does it matter where you go?"

I feel the weight of her eyes on me, considering. "What's the point in leaving if it isn't to someplace I want to be?"

"To get out?"

"But that's not the point. It's not *just* the point."

"I don't get it." Leaving is leaving. Who cares where you go if getting out is the goal? "If you don't like where you end up, you can just leave again, can't you?"

God, I sound like Mom.

Kat frowns, biting and releasing her lip. I catch myself staring and quickly redirect my attention toward the grass. This is starting to become a bad habit—looking at her.

"If I just went anywhere," she says, "because I don't want

to be here, I'd eventually feel how I do in Coldwater all over again. Sounds like a good way to be miserable for the rest of my life."

There's passion in her voice that bleeds into her accent, shaping the words on her tongue. She's put a lot of thought into this. So, I don't argue.

"What about you?" she asks. "Where are you heading off to?"

I lean back until we're sitting like parallel lines in the grass. "Nowhere yet. I've got another year. But then I want to go to Parsons. They've got a great photography program, and it's not just digital or film, it's everything. Video, installation, design, the perfect place where all of those things intersect." I smile. "I can learn so much."

"You sound excited."

"I am. But . . ." I sigh. "I need a photo project for my application. A portfolio. Something themed and cohesive. I was planning on doing that back home, finding the hidden gems of Jersey, I guess, but now . . ."

"Now what?"

Now I'm here. And I don't know this place at all.

I sigh. "Now I need a new idea."

"I'm sure you'll think of one," she says, and her voice holds more confidence than I feel.

Sitting in the grass next to Kat, soaking up the moonlight, is the most myself I've felt in Maryland so far. Her hand is near mine. I can feel it warming the grass, just as it warmed my palm when she dragged me through the party earlier.

And then my phone goes off. A loud buzzing in my pocket like a trapped mosquito.

I startle and reach for my phone. "James," I murmur in surprise, squinting at the sudden brightness of his face on my screen. The picture's from last year, one I took of him while we stood in line for a ride at the state fair. He's grinning at me over a giant blue-and-pink puff of cotton candy, strands of it stuck to his nose.

"Boyfriend?"

"Um." I hesitate. Why do I hesitate? "Yeah, boyfriend." The phone continues vibrating in my hand and my finger hovers over the screen. "He's going away to school, too. DC." Why does she need to know that?

Kat makes a noise of acknowledgment. Then she stretches, limbs long and languid, before standing. "I should head back. Don't want anyone setting anything on fire or falling off the roof."

I look up at her and she shrugs. "It's happened. Drunk people are assholes, but drunk, *bored* people are dangerous. Besides." She nods toward my phone. "I'll give you some privacy. You won't get lost out here, will you?"

I roll my eyes. "If I do, I'll just follow the bass back. Or the screams of someone who's just fallen off a roof."

She laughs as she walks away, glancing briefly over her shoulder at the woods. I wait for the sound of her to fade before I press decline on James's call.

ELEVEN

The attic is a sauna when I wake up. My head is still pounding with the lingering beats of club remixes, and my tongue is
stuck to the roof of my mouth. I grope blindly for my phone on
the nightstand and peer at it with blurry eyes until my brain
finally makes sense of Leslie's texts.

How was the party???

And then, right after: *You did go, didn't you? If you stayed
in your creepy little attic room, Jericka, I swear . . .* followed
by a flurry of emojis, most of which I'm not even sure I knew
existed.

Local Jersey girl doesn't turn into a wallflower at a party, I
respond. *Nation shocked.*

Her response is almost instant. Girl is always on her phone.

And?? Did you have fun?

I think of Kat. Of the way she looked in the dark, and
the movement of her braids over the grass. Of the strange
turns our conversation took and how easily we adapted, even

when ghosts were involved. It hadn't been fun, exactly, but I'd enjoyed myself. I'd been comfortable with her, which was more than I could say about the actual party.

James and the phone call I ignored come to mind.

It had its moments.

I stay in bed a little while longer, until the sun chases me out and downstairs for relief. The windows are open, and the fresh air is enticing enough that I nearly stick my head out the nearest one. There's no breakfast—Mom and Gram left for a checkup at the hospital twenty minutes ago—so I grab a banana from the bowl on the counter. I chew my first bite slowly, trying to imagine the two of them stuck in a hospital room together.

I'm still barefoot and crusty-eyed, but I head outside anyway. The breeze is generous, the sun surprisingly mild. I turn my face up to soak it in, happy with the midmorning quiet. I have no plans for the day. Freedom is a great feeling.

A honk cuts through the quiet when I'm halfway through my banana, loud enough to startle a brown-and-white kitten out of the crawl space, a small part of the family of strays that comes and goes. I turn toward the driveway. Kat's hanging halfway out of a tiny white car, waving. She's striding over to me before I can process it. We hadn't made plans. I didn't know she knew where Gram lived, and I haven't even brushed my teeth.

For a moment, I wonder how rude it would be if I ran inside to try and do that, but she's already standing in front of me.

"Hey," she says. Casual, as if we're just running into each other.

"What are you doing here?"

I just barely managed to pull my hair into something resembling a ponytail when I woke up, and I'm uncomfortably aware of the large T-shirt I wore to bed, covered in old bleach stains, and the half a banana in my hand.

"I came to see if you wanted me to play tour guide for you since I have the day off. I didn't have your number, so . . ." She shrugs. "Here I am."

"Here you are," I mutter. She looks great in a denim romper that cuts off midthigh. Her braids are piled haphazardly on top of her head, and a few strands have escaped to frame her face. She looks beautiful. It makes me feel worse.

"Is this a small-town thing?" I ask. "Showing up at someone's house first thing in the morning?"

"It's almost noon," she corrects me, "and I figured you wouldn't have too many other plans. So?" Kat raises her eyebrows. "Do you?"

"Have other plans or want to go with you?" What I want is to restart the day and take a shower the minute I wake up.

"Either."

I glance back toward her car. The tassel of a graduation cap hangs from the rearview mirror and the front bumper is scratched, but it looks mostly intact. "Does your car have AC?"

"It's a nice day out, I figured we could walk around, then hit up the diner. Town's only so big, and we'd miss most of it driving. Besides, I figured you'd wanna walk for picture-taking purposes and all. For your portfolio thing."

I'm flattered that she thought about my photography, but . . . "A nice day out? It has to be above eighty already."

She grins. "Like I said; it's nice out."

My hand tightens automatically around my banana. I relax as it starts to squish. "Sure, okay. Come inside? I need to . . ." Shower, brush my teeth, get dressed. "Get my life together."

Kat laughs and takes a seat on the porch, eyes locked on the crawl space kitten that's been watching us warily. "Go ahead. I'll wait out here. Hold up." She holds out her hand, palm up, and nods toward my banana. "Gimme."

"Would a 'please' kill you?"

"It might," she says, but she turns her gaze away from the kitten and toward me. A smile blooms on her face, bright enough that it coaxes one out of me. "Gimme," she says again. *"Please."*

I swallow hard, any reply I had sticking in my throat. I toss her the banana, careful not to touch her hand, and head inside to make myself decent.

◊

"So," I say as we head down the street and away from Gram's, "should I feel special or do you take every person new to Coldwater on a walking tour?"

Kat laughs, bumping into my shoulder. "Maybe it was the only excuse I could come up with to see you again."

Warmth that has nothing to do with the sun heats my

cheeks. My attraction to other girls isn't unfamiliar. I've known I was bi since I was twelve, but this feels different. Less a passing, appreciative glance, more the shock of a camera flash in the dark.

I don't know how to respond to her potential flirting, so I ignore it. "I take it no one fell off the roof during the party?"

I hadn't seen her again last night in the crush of bodies. By the time I dragged myself back inside, Asia was on the porch surrounded by friends and I hung out with them, fielding questions about New York until they got bored. Thinking of Asia makes my stomach hurt. While she was sober enough to drive me home, her tongue had been much looser than it was earlier that night.

"I can't believe you skipped the party to mope around with Kat," she said, tapping her fingers on the steering wheel to the beat of the song on the radio. "Just because people were at her house doesn't mean they like her, you know that, right? I mean, and it's not even the whole gay thing. That's whatever. Nobody *really* cares except old people and some of the assholes who're mad she won't sleep with them. I just mean, like, her whole ghost girl thing. It's weird."

She laughed. It was high and giddy and ended in a hiccup. "I'd figure she wouldn't wanna scare you off since you're the only person who's paid her any mind in ages, but I guess spreading her crazy's more important than trying to make friends. Unless . . . maybe *they're* her friends." She laughed again. "You should ask her if she talks to them! Ask her, and tell me what she says. *God*, I love this song . . ."

I shake my head, snapping back to the present.

"Nah. No casualties, anyway." She glances at me out of the corner of her eye. A smile pulls at her lips. "Good call with your boyfriend?"

Right. James. I grimace at the reminder. I haven't texted him to see what he wanted. I should do that. Eventually. "It went to voice mail before I could answer," I lie.

"Uh-huh," Kat says, and I ignore the way her smirk widens.

There are more hills here than I realized. After a few minutes, my calves have started cramping and I can feel myself getting winded. There are power line poles we have to skirt around every few feet, too, and proper farms with tractors parked close to the road and faded red barns straight out of a picture book. There are even a couple of horses. Behind a whitewashed fence, a light brown horse munches obliviously on grass. A smaller, paler one with an unruly black mane stands beside it, watching us.

I take a few pictures before continuing on. The quiet electricity I felt last night is back. It has me inching closer to her and taking my focus away from our surroundings, even when Kat's not saying anything or pointing things out. Still, it's hard for her to actually be a tour guide when there's not much to see. The houses are a mix of double-wides and old farmhouses that come in clumps of three or four. Kat points out who lives in each one, waving to the occasional person sitting on their front porch. Then it's back to open land, to wild grass and crops.

"Is your whole family from here?" I ask.

We're still walking along the road, but we could probably walk in the middle of it considering how few cars drive by. We're at least a mile from the house, but it's still visible in the distance like a sharp-eyed chaperone. The thought makes me smile.

"As far as I know. Some of my ancestors were freed slaves who weren't big into the whole sharecropping thing, so they went looking for something else and ended up here."

"Oh. Wow."

My family might have a similar history, but I don't know it. Mom acts like her history began the minute I was born.

"It feels like something I should be grateful for," she continues. "But mostly I'm just pissed no one ever decided they wanted to branch out any farther, you know?"

I nod but can't relate. If Kat's family has stayed rooted in place, mine has been constantly branching out. Away from here. Away from each other. "Leaving isn't always the answer," I point out. "It might be boring, but your history is here. And at least you've grown up being surrounded by it, having someplace to call home."

Kat shrugs. I don't think I've changed her mind, but I wasn't trying to.

We walk in silence for a few more minutes, until a large white building looms ahead. It's the biggest building I've seen besides Food Lion and the church. There are a handful of flags flapping lazily in the heat, but the American flag flies highest, nearly touching a power line.

"American Legion," Kat explains. "It's where all the old people gather to talk about Vietnam and how shitty our generation is." She laughs. "And it's where people throw birth-day parties and wakes after funerals. An all-purpose building."

It's small-town cute, like something you'd see in a Lifetime movie. "Did you ever have a birthday party there?"

She wrinkles her nose at me. "Sure have. Me and Wayne are only a couple weeks apart birthday-wise, despite the age difference, so every party we've ever had has been a joint birthday party. And they've all happened here."

Kat rolls her eyes when I laugh, and when we turn, I notice a building that seems out of place.

"What's that?" I ask.

That is a ruin of blackened wood and brick, half-crumbled and covered in dirt. It looks like something that belongs in the middle of the woods, not on a main town road. There are gaping holes like staring eyes where the windows and door should be. And the bell tower in the front is both bell-less and close to total collapse.

I don't give Kat a chance to answer me as I veer off our makeshift path and up the hill. It's no steeper than other hills we've climbed so far, but it's a struggle for some reason. Maybe it's the heat. This place is so different from anything else I've seen in Coldwater so far. Not a house or a trailer or a church or a barn. Just something old and alone.

My camera's in front of my face before I make the con-scious decision to put it there. My viewfinder fills with the strange ruin. Until Kat grabs my hand and pulls me away so quickly that all I can do for a second is blink at her blurry image in my lens.

"Don't."

I lower my camera with a frown. "Don't what?"

Kat doesn't answer me. She looks stuck, like she's seen the future and it's not just bad, it's horrific. Her grip on my hand is almost bone-crushing.

"Kat?"

She blinks her way back to the present and drops my hand. "My bad." She flashes me a grin that falls flat. "I just . . ." Her eyes drift back toward the ruin. "I usually avoid going this way. I wasn't paying attention."

"What is this place?"

"The old schoolhouse," she says quietly. "It's where all the echoes live."

TWELVE

Kat doesn't let us linger. In fact, she fidgets and grumbles and huffs while I take a few pictures, from a distance, until I give up trying to focus long enough for a good shot.

"Okay," I say finally. "Tell me. What's the deal with this place?"

"I don't want to talk here."

"Why—"

"Can we just go?" The words are sharp. She stands like she's one loud noise away from sprinting. She looks everywhere but at me.

"Okay . . . Should we head back to my house?"

"What? No. No, I . . ." She takes a deep breath. "I'm being the worst tour guide, aren't I?"

"Fits the town," I joke, and the furrow between her brows eases. "I'm willing to keep going if you are."

If it's just this place that's bothering her and whatever

ghosts she thinks live inside, I don't mind leaving. I can always come back and take pictures on my own.

"Let's go, then. We haven't even hit Main Street yet."

The last stop on our tour is the church. Or, more specifically, the tree behind it. It's huge, and in the shadow of the church graveyard, it's a symbol of life. It's not the biggest tree I've ever seen, but it's vibrant and my eyes are drawn to the quick flashes of color hidden in the leaves.

Kat gestures toward it with a flourish. "Ta-da. As far as tourist attractions go in Coldwater, this is my favorite. It's also the only one."

I stare at her. "It's a tree."

A pretty tree, blooming beautifully in the summer. But still.

"A bottle tree," she emphasizes.

I tilt my head back. "How come this one's different from yours?"

The tree at Kat's had bottles placed over its branches, jutting out so the branches trapped inside looked skeletal. The bottles on this tree, though, hang from string looped around its branches, swinging listlessly like wind chimes. Sunlight shines through them so the grass beneath glows blue and green. It's easy to imagine how people could believe these bottles trap spirits.

"Our tree's for keeping echoes away from the house. This one is to protect the town."

"Right," I say slowly. "From ghosts. Who have no bodies and probably can't touch anything or anyone."

"You say that like physical harm's the only kind there is." Her voice softens as she tilts her head back, staring up at the tree. "I think this is the quietest place in Coldwater. Anywhere else, I can hear them, even if it's just in the very back of my mind. But here, it's totally quiet."

I turn to her with a frown. "All the time? Even when you don't see them?" I don't believe in ghosts, but hallucinations are a real thing. "Look, Kat, maybe you should—"

She laughs. The smile she gives me is more amused than angry. "You probably think I'm crazy. Or just really good at long-term pranks."

"I—"

"I used to think so, too. That I was losing my mind or had a brain tumor or that I just had too much imagination, like my dad used to tell me."

"But?"

The breeze picks up and the sudden rush of wind sets the bottles swinging into one another. The air fills with the music of glass plinking against glass. It's surprisingly loud, and even when the wind dies down, the sound lingers.

For a moment, I think she won't answer.

Finally, she turns to me. "The schoolhouse was one of the first things built when Coldwater was founded. It was the town's pride and joy," she says. "A school, for a town full of newly freed slaves. What could be better to symbolize a brighter future? Even when the town grew and the land around here was settled and developed by white people who had more money to build bigger and better shops and schools, the old schoolhouse remained Coldwater's heart."

"Then there was a fire," I say, glancing back at the charred remains of the schoolhouse.

Kat nods.

"'Hell-sent,' my grandma used to say. It's how her mama described it to her and her mama before that: the opposite of heaven-sent. It was after school, so all the kids had gone home. But the teachers were there. It was meeting night, like it was every Wednesday, and every teacher, even the substitutes, was there. Half the women in Coldwater," Kat says, "and only a few of them ever came back out alive."

I stare at her. I've seen the after, but I can't help picture what the ruins might have looked like before the fire. Or during. "But what happened? What caused it?"

"It's all rumors. Anyone who knows for sure died in the fire or since. But . . ." Her frown deepens into a scowl. "A Freedmen's school had just opened in the town over. White teachers, white town, government in your business. Nobody paid it any mind because they didn't have to. Coldwater had what we needed—we could take care of ourselves. We didn't need anybody's help."

"Until the fire."

"Yeah," she agrees. "Until the fire."

The implications echo in my head, chiming like the clinking glasses above. Had the school really been burned down on purpose? I want the answer to be obviously no, but it's not too far-fetched by history's standards.

"So, you think all the echoes are . . . ?"

"Are the women who died," she confirms. "Coldwater did what it could to move forward. But half the town's women were dead and the schoolhouse was still there like a reminder. So, people started moving. They wanted to forget." Kat sighs. "I don't know if that's what made the echoes appear. All I know is that that's when people started leaving, and they haven't really stopped. The more people that leave, the stronger the chill and the noise gets. It's like the echoes are getting desperate. Like they're trying to hold on to the people still here." She snorts. "But it just feels like roots wrapped around my throat, keeping me so focused on breathing that even the idea of leaving is just wishful thinking."

I don't know what to say, or if I should say anything at all.

It's a good ghost story. It's a horrible real-life one.

If Kat's right, if everyone's leaving, then Coldwater's barely a town. Soon enough, there won't be anyone left. Just bottle trees and ruins and trauma shaped like a school.

Why not imagine ghosts exist here, then, to fill up all the extra space?

Her sudden laughter startles me. "Maybe I'm not cut out for the tour guide life. Apparently, all my fun facts are just depressing." She glances at me. "Ready to run away screaming yet?"

"Nah. I think I'll save that for if I run into any echoes." I smile. "I am hungry, though."

She relaxes, shaking off the weight of her story with a smirk.

"Yeah, I'm down to head to the diner. Hope you like grease and pancakes."

THIRTEEN

Kat fist-bumps the smiling crab on our way into the diner. It smells like maple syrup and dust inside, and the plastic seats cling to my thighs. We've taken a booth by the front windows. The tabletop is sticky with something I hope is syrup, and there's a tiny jukebox wedged between the ketchup and Tabasco on each table. The place is packed. There's a layer of chatter that joins the hum of the AC.

Things I learn about Kat at the diner:

- All of the waitresses call her Leen-Bean.
- Her mom used to work there.
- She doesn't like syrup on her pancakes.
- She hates scrambled eggs.
- She puppy-dog-eyes her way into tasting other people's food: home fries, in my case.
- She fidgets when she's sitting and rests

her legs on my side of the booth whenever she can.

- Out of all the songs on our booth's mini
jukebox, "(Sittin' on) the Dock of the
Bay" is her favorite.

We don't talk about echoes or the town's history, and whenever we fall silent, we listen to the music. Kat hums along to almost every song. She plays with the keys on the jukebox and listens to each sample like she can taste the music. Eyes closed, lips slightly parted to reveal the gap between her two front teeth, there's nothing but joy on her face.

I'm getting ready to tease her about it when two people, both about our age, slide into our booth. The guy crams him-self in on my side, scooting in far enough to push me toward the window. The girl slides in next to Kat, eyeing me from across the table.

"So, this is the New Girl everyone's been talking about. What, you planning on keeping her all to yourself, Kat?" the guy asks, grinning.

"No," she says, "but I sure as hell was planning to keep her away from you. What do you want, Will?"

Will laughs. "Can't I be friendly?"

She rolls her eyes, but doesn't actually seem upset. "Not without some other motive."

He holds up both hands. "Don't look at me. This is her fault," he says, nodding toward the girl.

The girl in question glares at him. Her hair is cut into a

curly black bob, and she has a round face that her cheekbones are lost in. There's a golden glow to her brown skin that makes me want to ask what moisturizer she uses.

"This is Mae," Kat introduces her, throwing an arm around the other girl's shoulder. "My best friend and occasional chaperone, like right now, apparently. Y'all come over here just to make sure I'm playing nice, or did you have an actual reason?"

Her accent is thicker than I've heard it, like it's dialed up to ten. I wonder if she tones it down with me or if it's just a subconscious thing. Either way, it's fascinating to listen to her, to watch the way her mouth shapes each word.

Mae smiles. Dimples appear in both her cheeks like tiny moons. "Mostly to bother you."

"We got news, too. There's a river party in a month or so," Will says. "First of the season." His excitement is almost endearing.

"What's a river party?" I ask.

"What's it sound like?" Mae's smiling, but her eyes are hard. They don't leave my face as she reaches for Kat's coffee and takes a sip without asking.

Kat nudges her. "A river party's like a house party and a beach party and a bonfire in one. People drink, dance, and hook up in trees. Set shit on fire and throw it in the water before it can spread. Y'know, small-town bullshit."

I don't know, but I nod along like I do.

"They're what everyone looks forward to in the summer. Them, and crab fests. You're coming, right?" Will glances back and forth between me and Kat, still grinning. "Kat brings all her girlfriends out there."

Girlfriends. I'm too flustered to be surprised by how casually Will says it, considering the stares and scrutinizing looks people have been shooting my and Kat's way since we got here.

My face flames. "Oh, no, we're not, uh," I stammer, but Kat laughs.

"She doesn't like parties. And she has a boyfriend," she assures him.

Mae makes a noise in the back of her throat. It sounds like doubt.

Lolly, the waitress, has just finished taking Will's and Mae's orders when Asia strides over. Her and two of her friends, girls from the party whose names I've already forgotten. They're all wearing some variation of the same crop top with shorts. Her sunglasses are perched on the top of her head, leaving her eyes free to glare at everyone until she stops on me with a smile too big to be real.

"I leave you alone for half a day and you've already gone and made friends with these fools? Sorry," she says before anyone can protest, "make that two fools and a ghost-obsessed lesbian." Her friends laugh. "Speaking of." She draws out the words as her smile grows. "You ask her yet?"

Kat stiffens and I don't know her well enough to tell whether it's anger or embarrassment. When she speaks, even her voice doesn't give it away. "Ask me what?"

"It's nothing," I promise. I turn to Asia. "Right, Asia? It doesn't matter."

"Then ask."

"It's honestly not a big deal," I urge. I can feel my heart beating in my palms.

Asia ignores me. If her grin was any bigger it'd split her face in half. "She wanted to know if you talk to those ghosts but mainly what the hell was wrong with you."

"I didn't—"

"I mean, I didn't tell her about your mom or the whole thing with the schoolhouse or how you didn't come to school for almost an *entire* quarter but—"

"Quit it, Asia."

Mae's voice is low but sharp. She's already on her feet by the time I turn to look at her. She has one hand on Kat's shoulder and the other balled into a fist at her side like anything Asia says next could be her last word for a while.

"I'm allowed to—" Asia starts.

"Yeah, she's allowed—" one of her friends adds, but Mae only narrows her eyes.

"I said quit." She raises her voice until it's audible over the music and the chatter and the AC. "Unless you want everybody in this diner to run and tell your mama about the time I drove you and Deonte up to Salisbury for—"

"Fine." Asia's quick to bite out the word. She forces a strained smile even as her eyes roam around. Everyone in this diner knows her. There probably aren't many secrets in Coldwater, but the ones that exist, including whatever it is that Mae knows, are probably fiercely kept.

"Fine," she says again. "Enjoy your lunch."

She stalks off without another word, friends flanking either side of her. Mae doesn't sit back down until all three are out of sight. As soon as they are, she turns her glare on me.

"What's your problem?"

I blink. My heart is still thumping loudly against my chest. The rush of blood in my ears is so loud. "*My* problem? I don't have one! She made that up."

She snorts. "Yeah, well, where there's smoke, there's fire. Asia's the worst, but she doesn't normally go outta her way to get to Kat. Whatever you said to her—"

"I didn't say anything!"

"—understand this. You can't be her friend and Kat's both. It doesn't work that way. I don't care if you're new; you know now. She's had enough to deal with—"

Kat hasn't quite thawed, but she's relaxed enough now to nudge her best friend. "Mae. Chill. I'm fine. If you want to be mad, save it for Asia."

To my surprise, Mae doesn't protest. Instead, she grabs the nearest drink and wraps her lips angrily around the straw, though she keeps glaring at me.

Will looks almost delighted, eyes bouncing back and forth between the three of us before landing on me. "Right, well, if nobody's said it yet: Welcome to Coldwater. Come for the ghosts, stay for the drama."

He pauses a second, then mutters to himself, "Damn, that's good. I should tag the welcome sign with that."

◊

Somehow, Kat and I manage to extricate ourselves from the diner before anything else happens. She gives me a rueful smile, hands in her pockets as we walk up yet another hill to head home.

"I'm sorry," I say, at the same time she says, "Sorry about them."

We laugh. Kat gestures for me to go first. I kick a rock that's in my path, and when it only rolls a few inches ahead, I kick it again. "I promise I wasn't talking about you with Asia. The last time I saw her, she was kinda tipsy and telling me things I should ask you about."

Kat shakes her head. "You don't have to apologize for Asia. I know how she is. I don't know if it's because of her crush on my brother or what, but the girl's had it out for me since third grade." She glances at me. "I should probably apologize for Mae, though."

"I don't think she likes me much."

"Don't take it personally. She barely likes Will and she's dating him." She laughs. "Henrietta Mae Wallace is prickly as hell, but only on the outside."

I study her face. My heartbeat has calmed, but the usual anxiety lingers. It mixes with dread as if the second this walk is over, Kat's never going to want to talk to me again.

"You're sure you're okay? I mean, even if you don't have to deal with her too often, nobody likes being singled out. Besides, you . . ." She had looked so blank, like she'd checked out completely. "You've just had a long day. You know, being questioned by a stranger for a couple hours and all."

She grins. "Your concern is very cute. But I'm more interested in whether or not my little tour changed your opinion of the town at all."

She called my concern "cute."

"I never told you my opinion in the first place."

"You said, and I quote, it was a 'shitty town.'"

Okay, so I was a little harsh. I put a hand over my heart sarcastically. "That latest field we walked past really changed my mind. I love this place. Ten out of ten."

She laughs, rolling her eyes. "I'll just have to keep trying. We can even take the car next time."

"Is this your way of letting me know you'll be showing up at my house again first thing in the morning?"

"It was noon," Kat reminds me as we approach the house. Mom's car is parked next to Kat's, gleaming silver in the sunlight. "And I won't have to if you give me your number."

I hold out a hand for her phone as I pass mine over, unlocking it so she doesn't see the lock screen photo of James. "Wow. Real smooth."

"I try."

I walk up to the porch door and pause, rocking back on my heels.

"Do you want to . . . come in?" What's the etiquette for inviting other people into someone else's house? I don't agonize over it for too long because Kat shakes her head.

"I gotta get going." She holds up her phone. "But I'll text you."

"Thanks," I say quickly because I realize I haven't yet.

"For the tour and, you know." For not washing your hands of me after everything with Asia. For telling me about the school-house. "Just getting me out of the house in general."

Her smile widens.

"Anytime," she says finally, and the warmth in her voice sparks a similar heat in my chest like joy made physical.

FOURTEEN

Despite having all weekend to prepare, I still feel like I'm going to puke by the time my dad comes to pick me up on Monday. I probably shouldn't be as nervous as I am. I'm not the first person in the world to meet new family members. In fact, on the scale of Meeting New People, this is like a four—I've at least talked to them on the phone, though the calls, as randomly as they come, always feel like the result of Cora's influence more than anything else. A ten would be being adopted and then meeting every biological member of my family at once, at a spur-of-the-moment family reunion.

It's not so bad when I put it that way. This is practically nothing.

Still. I want to throw up.

Every question I've ever had comes flying back into my head at once. *What are they like? Will they like me? After all these years, am I going to have an evil stepmother? Do those actually exist?*

If I talk, they'll all come spilling out in a rush, so instead I sit silently at the kitchen table listening to the groan of the porch steps and the creak of the screen door as my dad opens it to knock. I'm still sitting there at the second knock when Mom peeks her head in.

"You gonna get that?" she asks. I nod. I shake my head.

She heads for the door with a soft sigh. "Gerard." Her tone is neutral, professional. You'd never guess they had a baby together if I wasn't said baby.

"Lace."

The tension isn't as heavy as it was during his first visit, but it's still noticeable. I wipe my hand on my jeans and stand up.

"Hi . . . Dad." I cringe.

He smiles. "Ready to go?"

Not in the slightest. Still, my feet move on their own toward Mom to hug her goodbye. She squeezes me tighter than necessary. "Call me if you want to leave early or if—"

"She's not a baby," Dad interrupts. "She'll be fine."

Mom cuts a glare in his direction and squeezes me again. "Have fun. I love you," she says, taking a hesitant step back.

My dad's car is something burgundy and small with leather seats.

"Don't be nervous," he says as we pull out of the driveway. It's barely six o'clock and the sun is high enough in the sky to come pouring through the windshield. "Everyone's excited to meet you."

"Are they?" I ask doubtfully. "If I were in their position, I'd be less excited and more, I dunno, irritated." I've finally said more than two words since I've seen him and they weren't all questions. Progress.

"Irritated?"

"Yeah. I mean, here I come messing up family dynamics like some invasive species of . . . girl."

He frowns, fiddling with the radio. There doesn't seem to be a middle ground between static and country music. "You're not messing anything up. We've always considered you part of our family."

We. Our family. Sure, they have.

"Then how come—" I stop. No need to start off this visit with accusations, not when we're not even out of the car. Still, there's a bitter taste in my mouth, coating my tongue and all the questions resting on the tip of it.

"Then how come what?" He lets go of the wheel to wipe a hand on his jeans like he's nervous, too. "Go ahead and ask."

Thank God for door handles because my hand couldn't be wrapped tighter around it. "Then how come you never invited me here? Not for the summer or for holidays. Not for anything. I thought . . ."

I thought I didn't matter.

I thought he didn't give a damn about me except for when my birthday rolled around like a calendar reminder that, hey, I exist.

I thought I was over this a while ago.

He's quiet and I realize that he's waiting for me to finish my thought. I shake my head, knowing there's no nice way for it to end. He runs a hand over his bearded jaw. Maybe it's from him that I get all my fidgeting, not Mom.

"I did in the beginning. I mean, I asked your mom. But it was always too far—she would never drive back out here, and when I offered, she said she didn't want me knowing where you lived. I offered to meet halfway, but she said it was too much effort for the both of us."

"So, it's my mom's fault, then," I say flatly.

"No," he says, and there's something hesitant in it. "I could've kept reaching out. Asked you directly once you got older, but . . ." His jaw clenches. "But the older you got, the stranger it seemed for me to try and connect with you when I didn't have a clue who *you* were."

He huffs a laugh. "Sounds like an excuse, I know, but I'd known exactly who you were before you left. I knew that you hated cream cheese on bagels but loved it on toast instead of butter. I knew you were scared to death of butterflies and that your favorite spot to hide during hide-and-seek was the upstairs bathroom closet. I knew you liked being tickled but hated when anyone touched your feet and that you'd scream to high heaven if I tried to do your hair but were sweet as cream when Cora did it."

He sighs. "I used to know all that and it was hard, I guess, admitting that I knew nothing about you since."

I'm quiet, thinking of all the things he remembers about me that I don't remember about myself. "You've been with Cora that long?" I ask after a while.

He glances at me, a small smile on his lips. "Yeah. She

kept me sane when you were going through your terrible twos. She's a good mom. She was a great mom to you."

I frown. "You mean, like on the weekends?"

"Yeah," Dad says after a pause. He keeps his eyes on the road and firmly away from mine. "On the weekends." A car drives by and honks at us; he honks back.

"They really are excited to see you," he says.

◊

Someone's crying when we walk through the door. The house isn't large, but it's bright. The living room walls are painted a cheerful orange, the couch is littered with yellow cushions, and even the kids' toys scattered around add to the decor. The house looks lived in. Cozy. And it smells like spaghetti.

A little girl sits on the floor. She's the one crying. Mario Kart is on-screen and the boy sitting on the rug next to her, shimmying in victory, is clearly the winner.

"Kya, fix your face, it's just a game. Marcus, I swear if you're in there being a sore winner, I will—Oh!" A curvy woman in an apron comes into the living room, brandishing a wooden spoon in one hand, and stops short when she sees me.

Cora.

She laughs. It's low and throaty and self-deprecating. Her mouth is wide, her teeth a little crooked when she beams at me. There's a small trail of moles down her neck that remind me of ants marching along a sidewalk. She puts a hand to her heart.

"Look at you," she says, and to my horror it sounds like

she's near tears. "You're here and all grown-up. I told Gerard you'd be a cute one." She starts forward and then stops herself, her hands falling to her sides. "Mind if I give you a hug?"

I nod. It's a quick, warm squeeze, and I get a whiff of coconut and palm seed oil that sends me headlong into a memory.

Sit still a spell, Jelly Bean. Let me finish up this last braid.

I blink hard and it's gone as quickly as it came, leaving my ears ringing. "Did you say something?"

Cora cocks her head slightly but only smiles. "Just that I've missed you something fierce."

"Right," I say. "Yeah."

Kya and Marcus stop their crying and dancing to stare at me. Marcus looks like his mom; they have the same wide face set between tiny ears. Kya, though, looks a little like pictures of me when I was younger, with an overbite and round eyes, right down to the barrettes weighing down the ends of her twists. It's weirdly gratifying confirmation that we're related.

"Go on," Cora says to them. "Say hi to your sister."

Sister. What a weird word.

Marcus waves.

Kya smiles shyly.

I mutter a hello.

And then we resume our awkward, fascinated staring until Marcus grins at me. He looks like a little brother should—like he's a bit of a troublemaker. "Wanna lose in Mario Kart?"

Which is how I spend the first half of the night: losing to my siblings on Rainbow Road repeatedly.

◊

The second half is more what I expect. We sit at a table that looks like a slab of wood in the middle of a plain dining room, with Dad and Cora across the table and Kya and Marcus on either side of me. Kya's pulled her chair as close to me as she can get without sitting in my lap and Marcus has already made me switch spots.

In the middle of the table is a bowl of spaghetti, a smaller bowl of Parmesan, a bottle of hot sauce, and salt and pepper shakers shaped like pandas. Cora slaps Marcus's hand lightly when he reaches for the hot sauce. He grins when I look at him.

For about a minute, there are only the sounds of forks scraping plates and people slurping noodles. Dad shoots glances at me in between bites of food. Cora breaks the silence first.

"How's your grandmother doing? And your mama?"

It feels wrong that she should ask about Mom. Weird, even though it's obvious she's being genuine. "They're fine," I say, busying myself with twirling spaghetti around my fork.

"Must be strange, her being back after so long."

Is she fishing for something? I glance at her, but she only smiles sweetly. I look away, ignoring the urge to smile back.

"I guess. Probably weirder for me since I've never been here. Or don't remember it, anyway."

When I look at her again, she's sipping iced tea and there's something sad in her eyes that reminds me of the car ride with

Dad. Whatever I don't remember, it's clear that she does. *Jelly Bean.*

My heart creeps its way down to my stomach, taking up space for any appetite I'd had. This is what I hadn't wanted: awkward, stilted conversation; attempts at politeness and connection. But it's hard to avoid when every question asked only fuels the desire to ask my own. When there's history that Cora and Dad are obviously trying their best to tiptoe around.

Across from me, he clears his throat. He picks up and sets down his fork enough that I'm starting to think it's a tic. Cora places a gentle hand atop his, and when he opens his mouth to speak, I see her give it a squeeze. When he looks at her, she shakes her head. With a free hand, he picks up his glass and drains the rest of his iced tea.

"How old are you?" Kya asks suddenly, pulling my attention away. She's been watching me in between bites, too, trying, it seems, to gauge whether or not I'm big sister material.

"Seventeen," I say. "How old are you?"

"She's seven," Marcus chimes in. "But I'm way older. I'm ten."

"It's not a competition, Mar." Dad chuckles. He says it softly, affectionately enough that it must be a familiar thing between the two of them. Marcus smiles.

And I feel it instantly, like a kick to the gut. Jealousy.

This is what it would've been like to grow up with my dad—to know him at all. Family dinners and inside jokes and warmth. Probably not all the time, but sometimes is better than never.

The conversation moves on to other things. Kya's dance classes and upcoming recital; a movie that they all saw in Salisbury; a new video game Marcus keeps begging for. I smile and nod when I should, remembering to take bites of spaghetti that mostly tastes like garlic powder and red pepper. I should be focused on getting to know everyone, but Dad's words in the car keep playing on a loop in my head.

It was hard, I guess, admitting that I knew nothing about you since.

Wasn't parenting supposed to be hard? Did he not think it had been hard for me, too?

I'm psyching myself out, putting too much weight onto this one dinner. I know I am. But I can't help it. One dinner doesn't make up for fourteen years without them. How does he expect me—how do I expect *myself*—to be able to do this like it's nothing?

I set down my fork and it clatters against my plate louder than I mean for it to. Kya looks at me, a noodle poking from between her lips, with sauce splattered on her cheeks. Dad wipes it away with a napkin. He's probably done that for her a million times. He's probably tucked her in at night or yelled at her when she was in trouble or picked her up at school when she wasn't feeling well. She's never known what it's like to not have both parents there. To have some sort of frustrating phantom pain where one parent should be.

I push my chair back and stand. "Excuse me," I say. "I need some air."

I retrace my steps until I'm back at the front door, ignoring the pictures and milestones lining the walls. I don't want to see their happy family; I've had enough of being on the outside. I hear Marcus and Kya behind me, asking Cora whether I'm leaving already and if they can have dessert, but the door shuts on her reply.

I sit on the porch swing out front, all white wood and bright blue cushions. It's cute. I can imagine Kya and Marcus swinging from it, their feet dangling. Dad and Cora snuggling to watch a sunset. Jealousy is an uncomfortable sensation, like swallowing ice whole. I wouldn't trade the life I had with Mom for this one, but it doesn't stop me from wondering about the kind of life we might have had here, with Dad.

The door creaks open. A moment later the swing dips beside me with added weight. I don't look at Dad and he doesn't speak.

When the sun slips below the tree line, I ask, "Why didn't you fight harder to stay in my life?" He's quiet, so I keep going. Anger's surging in me like bile. It's even more uncomfortable to swallow, so I don't bother trying. "Lots of things are hard. Calculus, learning how to drive, applying to colleges. And guess what? I still have to do all of those things! I still have to *try* to do them! But apparently you can just pretend like you don't have a daughter whenever you feel like it!"

"Jericka—"

"No. I want to know what that's like, knowing I exist and not bothering to have anything to do with me. Because I know how much it hurts for me. But how is it for you? Is it embarrassing, now that you have these cute, perfect kids and a cute, perfect family? Is it—"

"Awful," he says quickly, his voice hushed. "It's awful." I go silent in surprise. "I think about you constantly, Jericka. About when you lived with me and Cora and about how you left and how I let you go. And that's the awful part. That I didn't fight for you then and haven't fought for you since. This whole night, hell, since Friday, it's the only thing I've been able to think about."

"What are you talking about? When did I live with you and Cora?"

Dad's eyes are steady on mine. "When your mom left, we—"

"When she *left*?" I shake my head. "She never left me. We moved away together."

"You were just a baby. A couple months old." His voice is soft, comforting, but I don't want to hear him. We were just talking about him abandoning me.

I shake my head again but he keeps talking. "She loved you, of course she did, but she didn't really . . . take to you. She was scared; we both were. We were barely older than you are, and babies are scary." He chuckles a little. "They scream and they're demanding and they don't let you take breaks. It can get overwhelming."

He sighs. "But this is a settling town. It was created to be a place of permanence for people to put down roots, live out their days. That's what you do here. You settle."

I don't care, I think. *I don't care, I don't care.* I want him to get on with whatever he's trying to tell me before this rush of anxiety and fear makes me collapse.

"Mom isn't the settling type, I know," I snap. "So, what?"

"So, I could never compete with the world. She wanted to be out in it too badly. And after she had you . . . that longing to get out hit her a little harder."

I inhale slowly as my chest tightens. "So, she left."

"There was more than just you and me here. There were memories, you know? Plenty of good, but—"

"It's just a yes or no question. Did she leave me or not?"

It takes too long for him to answer. His eyes look faraway, as if he's back in that moment. Back in his eighteen-year-old body watching his ex-girlfriend deliver his infant daughter and all her stuff to his door. "She didn't want to leave when you were old enough to remember her going."

"How long was she gone?"

"Jericka, you have to understand—"

"I don't have to do anything!" My hand wraps tight around the chain of the swing. The cool metal is a lifeline. My stomach is churning. "Just answer the question, please. *How long was she gone?*"

He sighs deeply. "She came back when you were three. That's when you moved away."

Three years.

Three. Entire. Years.

I shut my eyes. I can feel myself trembling, feel the swing

rocking beneath me, but none of it feels real. Everything feels secondary. Even the bile in my throat and the headache behind my eyes could belong to someone else.

Three years. I think my dad is saying something, but I can't hear him. What kind of follow-up could he give that would make any of this better?

I open my eyes. The sun has completely set and the dark is a new, interested party in our conversation. Crickets begin their chirping. The night is loud.

I'm thankful it keeps our faces hidden from one another.

"Just know you meant *everything* to me, Jericka. And I had to let you mean everything to your mom, too, for a while."

For a while. I stand abruptly, the swing jostling forward to hit the backs of my legs. I need movement. I feel like if I don't move, I'll scream, and if I scream, I'll never stop.

"Fourteen years isn't a while," I say, pacing the length of the porch. "It's a lifetime. It's *my* lifetime. And why would you—I mean, how could you—?"

I stop in front of him. Cora must have turned the porch light on sometime during my pacing because we're face-to-face now, both of us painfully visible. Me and Dad, with his sad, dark eyes and his crooked nose and his graying beard. If he's telling the truth, I'd probably known that face better than my own, once.

Now it's just like looking at a stranger.

A stranger who decided to blow up my reality.

"Why did you tell me this? Why now?"

What had Mom missed during those years? I can't help but think of Cora and her warm smile and the easy comfort she radiates. Had I considered her my mom once? Had I been scared to leave her and go with Mom?

"It felt wrong to sit there and eat dinner and act like we hadn't done this before hundreds of times. I didn't want you to feel like we didn't care about you."

"No," I say. I can hear the bitterness in my voice. "Just that my mom didn't."

"I'm not trying to blame her. I just—"

"No, go for it. She left, right? Blame her all you want!" I start my pacing again in earnest. "She's such a hypocrite, judging Gram when she's not any better. At least Gram had a reason and it wasn't just that she was tired of being a mom. At least she lasted a few years, not just a couple of months." My voice breaks but I refuse to cry. I'm sick of this ebb and flow of emotion. I want anger to stay. I want it to fuel me. To let me hurt them as much as I've been hurt.

"Jericka." There's a note of warning in Dad's voice now. "Watch yourself. She's still your mother."

I laugh. It's a high-pitched thing that belongs among the crickets and cicadas. "She's a liar. And so are you. No wonder you guys hooked up so young."

I turn away from my dad, toward the front yard and everything beyond it. I'm suddenly eager to be lost in the dark.

"I need to go."

He stands. "I'll drive you."

Drive me where? Back to Gram's, where I'll have to face

Mom? Back to Jersey, where she built up a life and a past for me to erase the one she hadn't been part of?

"No. I'll walk."

I can feel his eyes on me as I jog down the porch steps, walk toward the road, first alongside it, then right in the middle. There are no streetlights, but there are also no cars. No one to see me, no one to see.

Don't let me go, I think. *Not again.*

I listen for the sound of his footsteps trailing me or the engine of his car. I hear neither. I wait a few minutes. Then I take out my phone to text the only person I know in Maryland who hasn't lied to me.

FIFTEEN

I'm pacing the side of the road, kicking up dust and dirt, when the temperature drops. The second I turn around, I'm lost. I don't even have time to look at the echo properly before her eyes are on mine, holding me in place. It's like the moment before you jump into a pool, that split second of surface tension where you're aware of the air on your face and then everything is water.

It's a slip from the present to something present-shaped. First here. Now elsewhere.

Everything hurts.

It's a pain so deep that there's no beginning or end. All of it is mine, but the intensity is wrong. It's *more*. More than I felt walking off the porch, more than every way I've ever been hurt combined. The pain is sharp enough that I can taste it. It tastes like outside. Like dirt and grass and, strangely, smoke.

One person shouldn't feel all of this, I think.

It's a wonder I can still think at all.

Stay.

The echo holding my gaze is more outline than person. Through the haze, I can just barely make out her face. She's an old woman with a sharp chin and wrinkles so deep her cheekbones are lost in them.

Stay.

The word burrows, vibrating, beneath my skin.

The echo's eyes fill with tears. Her mouth is shut, but I hear it again. Like a hum.

Stay.

And again.

Staystaystaystaystaystaystaystaystay
Staystaystaystaystaystaystaystaystay
Staystaystaystaystaystaystaystaystay
Staystaystaystaystaystaystaystaystay
Staystaystaystaystaystaystaystaystay
Staystaystaystaystaystaystaystaystay

I don't know if what I'm feeling is my pain or hers. Maybe it doesn't matter. We're stuck in this loop and I don't know how to end it.

Maybe I can't.

"Just let me go," I whisper.

She opens her mouth, but headlights shine straight through her before she can say anything. *Stay* softens to a whisper, but it doesn't disappear completely.

"Hey." Kat's voice. Not the echo's. She's sticking her head out the window of her car, all but invisible between the glare and the darkness. "You might want to get the hell inside before more come."

SIXTEEN

"Do you want to talk about it or do you just want me to drive?" Kat asks.

I'm in the passenger seat of a car that smells nauseatingly like bubble gum, watching a stuffed bird hanging from the rearview mirror twirl in slow circles around the graduation cap tassel. The only question Kat asked when she texted me back was where I was. When I hadn't been able to answer, she'd told me to hold tight. So, I feel like I owe her some explanation. When I try, though, all that comes out is . . .

"What the hell?"

"Okay, I guess you need a minute to process."

"A *minute*? Try an hour. Or a month. Or, I dunno, maybe the rest of my freaking life!"

"I did warn you."

I snort. "Are you really 'I told you so'-ing me right now?"

"If I wanted to do that, I'd just say *I told you so*."

I shut my eyes and let my head fall back against the seat. "I didn't believe you."

"I know."

"I thought you were crazy."

"I figured."

"I thought it was weird and kind of interesting, but I didn't really think you were serious, you know?" I groan. "I mean, ghosts? Here? *Really?*"

She laughs, but I can barely hear her over the sound of my racing heart and the pounding in my head. "Really."

I go quiet, too many thoughts bouncing around at once. Kat focuses on driving. The radio plays an old R&B song on low. It's barely eight but there's no one else out, so the night feels ancient.

"Tell me something," I say suddenly.

"Like what? A ghost story?"

I ignore her teasing. "Anything. Please."

Between my dad's confession and my first echo run-in, I'm not sure which is worse. Both have my mind in turmoil, both are responsible for my shaking hands and racing heart. My head feels like it might split in two.

"I learned how to drive on the back roads when I was fourteen," Kat says after a moment. "With Wayne, because my dad was too scared to teach me himself. Smart, really." She laughs. "I hit a tree stump during my first lesson and nearly swerved off the road and into a ditch. In my defense, though, those back roads are brutal. They're mostly dirt, and if a tree falls in the middle of one? Too damn bad, I guess. They're the kind of roads you just have to know by heart and play it safe until you do. Unfortunately for my dad's car, I didn't know that yet."

Kat grins. "My dad's not the angry type, but you should've seen his face when we brought his truck back. Wayne was grounded for a month. I got off with a warning because, hey, I wasn't the licensed driver in the car."

I turn to Kat. The soft indent of a single dimple is on full display as she smiles at the memory. "Considering I'm sitting in your car, I'm guessing you got a lot better?"

"Guessing or hoping?" She laughs. "I'm good enough to have a license, anyway. Which isn't saying much in Maryland."

A smile tugs at the corners of my lips despite myself. "Yeah, well, after tonight I think I've learned to take you at your word."

"You oughta."

"I appreciate it."

"My driving?"

"The distraction. Tonight has been . . ." My voice wavers and I pause to get it under control. "Well. It hasn't been great."

She nods. She doesn't ask what's wrong. I appreciate her even more. "We've got a good amount of night left. You want me to drop you off at home?"

"No." I say it too sharply. Too quick. Just the thought of seeing my mom makes my headache worse.

She glances at me. "I can keep driving, but we'll run outta

gas. And if you hadn't guessed, there aren't any all-night gas stations out here."

"I don't need to drive around all night," I promise. "Just for now."

We're ahead a few miles and a few minutes when I speak again. "Kat?"

"Yeah?"

"Could you tell me another story?"

She launches into one with barely any hesitation, something about her tenth birthday party and Wayne's thirteenth. I zone out before the party even begins. My newfound fear of the dead has faded to a steady, dull roar, leaving me just enough space to sift through every interaction with Mom in search of lies. Can she see the echoes, too? Had they asked her to stay? Were they all she heard while she was packing to leave me, a chorus she was trying to outrun?

Was it actually her I went to the first time I had the recurring nightmare about the bees? Was it the smell of her cooking or Cora's that lives in my very first memory, where only my tiny, chubby feet are visible and the taste of something delicious fills my mouth? And what's wrong with me that I could've forgotten the people who raised me and replaced all my memories with the woman who didn't? Three years isn't insubstantial. Even if I can't remember, Dad and Cora's influence must still be in the way I say certain words, in the gestures I make, in the foods I like.

Or has Mom usurped them completely—cemented her stolen place as number-one parent?

My head pounds. I feel like I'm . . . lacking. Like someone pickpocketed me in a crowd and walked away before I even had the chance to notice.

"What was it like when your mom left?" I ask suddenly. I'm not entirely sure I haven't interrupted her midstory.

We both wince as the car jolts, hitting a deep pothole. She straightens us out, and when she speaks her voice is carefully neutral. "What, besides shitty?" When I nod, she sighs. "I dunno what you want me to say. It was confusing and scary. I'd only ever spent a week away from her before then, when I went to Ocean City with my grandparents. But I still knew she was at home waiting for me."

She sighs. "Mom and home are the same thing when you're that age, you know? That was the hardest thing to get through my head, after. That whenever the school day was over, she wasn't going to be there."

"Did you ever see her again?"

"Yeah. She came to Wayne's high school graduation. She texts when she wants. Calls. I don't usually answer. What's there to say?" She shakes her head. "Why'd you ask?"

I stare past the windshield. I try to think of how to explain everything I'm still failing to process. "My mom left, too."

"Obviously. That's why everyone's gossiping about her being—"

"No. She left *me*." Somehow, it's worse saying it out loud.

I tell her everything Dad told me. Partly because I think she'll understand, partly because I'm not ready to go back to Gram's.

"Shit," she says finally. "So, what are you gonna do about it?"

"Do?"

"Town's only so big. I can only drive you around so many times."

"If we keep driving, maybe I'll think of something."

She laughs, then presses harder on the gas, and we jolt forward with a burst of speed.

SEVENTEEN

When I finally check my phone, there's a text from Dad asking if I got home okay, and multiples from Mom.

Door's unlocked when you get home.

We're heading to Peninsula Medical.

Might stay overnight.

I turn to Kat. "What's Peninsula Medical?"

"Hospital over in Salisbury." She glances at me. "How come?"

I swallow and read the text aloud. Mom didn't say what was wrong, but it must be something serious if they're going to another town's hospital this late at night. I hear my breath cut through the silence, shallow and too quick. Kat must hear it, too, because she reaches over to touch my knee without taking her eyes off the road.

"It'll only take us twenty minutes to get there, okay?"

I nod. I would thank her if I could speak, but worry and

fear are holding my voice hostage. I focus on breathing. In. Out. In. Out.

In.

What if Gram dies before I get the chance to know her? What if she's already dead?

Out.

I think of the advice she gave me. I think of my anger at her, my suspicion, and of whether it's unfounded and unfair. I think of all the years she spent on her own and how, when she knew it was the end, she came back here because she didn't want to be alone. Somehow, it seems less selfish than it did before. Now it just seems like a reasonable thing to want. Family. Connection. A bit of familiarity.

Why did I bother trying to start getting to know her when she's about to die?

"Hey," Kat says, coaxing me out of my thoughts. "We're almost there. You okay?"

No. No, I am not okay. My world seems determined to twist upside down as many times as possible in one night.

And how am I supposed to even look at Mom, let alone act like everything is fine, now that I know the truth?

I wrap my hand around the door handle and squeeze. "I'll be fine," I say. "I'm sorry I dragged you out here."

"Don't mention it. I wasn't doing much."

For the first time, I wonder what she'd been doing when I texted her and why she dropped everything for me. I try to hold on to the image of Kat sitting in her bedroom, reacting to my text, but it's swept away in the quick-moving tide of more pressing thoughts.

"Do you think she's dead?" I ask. "She seemed fine before I left. She seemed fine this whole weekend. Can cancer really move that fast?"

I'm rambling, but I'm not sure what else to do. There *isn't* much else to do.

"Hopefully you'll find out when you get inside," Kat says. Somehow her voice is calm. Then again, her grandmother's not the one dying.

She pulls up to the emergency entrance a minute later and shifts into park. She turns to look at me in the red glow of the emergency sign. "Good luck in there."

◊

It's not until I'm at the front desk that I realize I don't know Gram's last name. I'm trying to explain this to the reception-ist, but she only smiles at me in that pitying way reserved for funerals and hospitals.

She's quiet as she looks Gram up by her first name. "Carol Annette Simms," she says, with emphasis on the last name that matches Mom's. "Room 525. Elevators are to your right."

The elevator is fast. I barely have time to imagine all of the awful things I could be walking into by the time it reaches Gram's floor. Her room is easy to spot, made easier by Mom sitting cross-legged outside the door. I'm unprepared for the flood of emotions I feel at seeing her.

Fear for Gram.

Anger for everything I've learned tonight.

Worry and abandonment and betrayal.

So much love it hurts.

I look at her, then back toward the door, and the surge of panic in me dissolves everything else. "Why are you out here? Where's Gram? Is she—"

"They're checking her now," Mom says quickly. "Jericka, she's fine. Calm down. What are you doing here? How did you get here?"

"You can't just text people that you're going to the hospital and then expect them to be calm or not show up!"

I'm yelling. Logically I know that's Not Acceptable by hospital standards, but I can't seem to lower my voice.

"Come here," Mom says, standing and holding out her arms like she's expecting me to take my first steps into them. I never did, I realize dully. "Come sit."

"I don't want to sit with you," I mutter. I lean against the wall across from her and let myself slide down onto the linoleum.

"I didn't mean to worry you," she says, mimicking my actions. "How did you get here? Did your dad—"

No. I don't want to talk about Dad right now. If I talk about Dad, I will go back to yelling.

"A friend dropped me off. What happened?"

"I don't know," she says. She sounds tired. "She kept coughing and she's having trouble breathing. She had a fever. I wasn't sure what to do . . ." She trails off and draws her knees up to her chest. She rests her forehead on them. "I called Miles. Not that there's anything he can do from Georgia, but, I thought, just in case. He told me where her inhaler was and to bring her here if it didn't help. Funny, he's better at this whole thing than I am."

I squash the bitter laugh welling up in my chest and glare at the wall next to her. *I know*, I want to say. *You only care about yourself.*

"I'm glad you're here," she says, turning her head, still on her knees, to smile at me. "You should've stayed home, but still."

Something tightens in my chest and in my throat. Tears are imminent. "I'm gonna go check on her."

I bump into a doctor on her way out. She gives me a strained smile. There are circles like bruises beneath her eyes, and it feels later in this hospital than it does outside. Like everyone here has gone days without sleep. "Will she be okay?" I ask.

"She has an infection and she'll need to stay for a few days to make sure nothing gets worse. But, yes. She's stable for now."

For now. Doctors shouldn't be allowed to say things that sound so ominous.

Gram's sitting up at an incline. She looks older since the last time I saw her. There are wires and IVs sticking out of her, connected to a number of beeping machines.

"Don't come in here asking me how I'm feeling," she warns. "I'm not planning on dying tonight and not from no damn cold."

A series of coughs rack her body and the bed underneath

as I perch on the edge. When they subside, the breath she pulls in has a slight wheeze. She pushes the remote toward me. I flip through until she tells me to stop.

"You trying to get rid of us already?" I ask as lightly as I can. My eyes are fixed on the screen, some old episode of *Divorce Court*. The judge has short red hair and she looks irritated whenever either party speaks. "You dying means we'll be heading back home."

Home. It's a throwaway word now more than it is a place with sentiment behind it.

"Should be glad, then. It ain't hard to guess you both don't want to be here."

Gram's voice is teasing, but I twist around to frown at her. "But we *are* here."

"Yeah," she says. "You are."

I take a deep breath. "I'm sorry about what I said before. That you should have dealt with this on your own." I shake my head. "That was mean. Nobody should have to be alone when . . ." I trail off. Nobody should have to be alone, period. Not when they don't want to be.

Gram grunts. "Been alone plenty."

"Now you're not."

She cracks a smile. I offer one back. I don't know what this is between us. All I know is that it's something kindred and wary and small, calming everything else still raging wild beneath my skin.

EIGHTEEN

"What's wrong?" Mom asks finally. "Something's been bothering you since last night at the hospital."

I crack my window. I breathe in grass and car exhaust.

Mom sighs. "What's the problem, Jericka?"

I try my best not to snap at her. I really, really do. But there's no tactful way to tell your mother that you know she abandoned you as an infant. "My problem," I whisper, because I don't dare yell, "is that you gave me up and then snatched me away and you never bothered to tell me about any of it."

I watch her hands. The one on the wheel goes slack, but the one resting on her thigh stays perfectly still. "I don't regret it," she says. She doesn't even hesitate. "I know what kind of mother I would have been if I hadn't left. I needed that time to myself to learn who I was as a person before I could figure out who I was as a mother."

"Did you practice that?" I ask before I can stop myself.

"Have you spent years perfecting the answer you'd give when I finally found out?"

She laughs. *Laughs.* "Try days. Gerard can't hold water, so I figured it was only a matter of time."

I chew my cheek so I don't grind my teeth. "Fourteen years is a long time."

"He never called enough for it to be much of an issue."

"Are you serious?" My entire body throbs. "Are you blaming him for not calling? For not being the one to keep in touch? He's not the one who left—"

"You don't know what you're talking about."

"Then tell me! After all this time, don't I deserve the truth? Were you ever going to tell me?"

"You didn't need to know."

"I didn't need to know?" I raise my voice. "I didn't need to know that my entire life has been built on a lie about how it was just me and you, that we were a unit, that we grew up together and—"

Her hand tightens around the wheel. "It *is* just me and you."

"No, it's not! *I* have a family. One that you ripped me from because you were *selfish*—"

"You were mine—"

"I'm not a gift, Mom! I can't be given and then taken back whenever you feel like—"

"But you were." Her voice goes soft. "You were a gift." She takes a deep breath. For the first time, I see her hands shake. I've surprised her with this, rehearsed answer or not.

After a few minutes, she drifts toward the side of the road and parks the car. We're nowhere that I recognize, but there's a small sign out my window. It's pale blue, the letters a faded white, and every inch of it is covered in dust.

COLDWATER, it declares itself in all capital letters. And underneath, in tiny print: *Restoring and Cherishing Our History*.

She gets out, heads around to the trunk, and hops on top, patting a spot beside her to join her, and after a beat, I do. The metal is hot on the back of my thighs but not unbearable.

"You don't know what it's like to feel trapped," she says. "I've tried to make sure of that. Better to get used to something new than to grow numb to the same nothing happening on a loop around you. That's what it was like growing up here."

Mom sucks her bottom lip between her teeth. "Every day, I wanted to leave. There was nothing for me here and so much just past this sign. A whole world out there, where maybe the days would feel like they were actually moving."

She turns to me. Her expression softens the way it does when she's about to cry. "Then I had you. And the days started moving. But you were so little. And you needed so much."

She laughs. "You cried constantly, and I cried every time you did. And in the middle of all of that, this town never *shut up*." She squeezes her hands together so tightly I'm afraid something will break. "When the doctor gave you to me for the first time, Jericka, I have never felt more human. But I had also never felt so scared. Scared that I'd fail you. That I couldn't be the mother you deserved. I thought it would get better as you got older. But it only got worse. And the town made sure I knew that now that you were here, I really couldn't go anywhere. I had double the obligation to stay. Everyone was watching me, waiting to see if I'd be like my own mama and disappear."

"So, you decided to prove them right?"

"No. I made a choice for both of us. Right here by this sign. You were with your dad and I was alone for what felt like the first time in so long. I thought maybe Gerard could handle everything better. He and Cora were Coldwater to the core: They weren't in a rush to go anywhere. This was their home, and they'd stay and do what was expected of them without question."

She points at something across the road. At first, I think she's pointing at the woods. But then I see them. Echoes. Not just one but a handful. None of them look at us, but I stiffen anyway. Mom sighs.

"I know you've seen them. Last night, I could tell. Everyone that has gets this . . . air about them. Something in the eyes goes permanently sad." She frowns. "I thought I'd become one of them if I stayed," Mom says. "It's a silly thought, no one who's died since that fire ever has, but sometimes, I still think it."

"Then why come back at all? Even for me?"

"Because I love you. And because I realized that when I left you behind, I trapped you, too. I wanted you out. I didn't want you playing tag in the yard with women who died decades ago or getting used to this town tugging at you with every step."

"That wasn't your choice to make, though. You should've let me decide."

"Jericka." My name is a whisper in her mouth. "That's exactly what I was trying to do."

I squeeze my eyes shut. "Yes, but . . ."

In trying to give me a choice, she didn't give me one at all.

"But what about everyone else?" I ask.

"Everyone else wasn't my problem. I didn't care about everyone else."

I open my eyes and frown. "But they cared about me." Hadn't they? Dad and Cora, my grandparents and any other family I'd had once? "I wasn't just yours."

Mom smiles softly. "Of course you are. What would you rather I'd done? Left you here forever?"

"How about not leaving me in the first place?"

"Oh, baby. Everyone leaves sometimes. It's the coming back that matters."

NINETEEN

"Your mama told me you've seen one of 'em. Not everybody can."

It's the first thing Gram says as she carefully lowers herself down next to me on the porch steps a few days later. It's not hard to guess who she means.

"Yeah. Guess you have, too?"

She hums. "Runs in the family, it seems. The women, anyway."

"Lucky us."

We fall into silence, but I have a million questions I want to ask, starting with: Why us?

"Why'd you really come back?" I ask instead.

"Thing about a question," she says, "is there's usually more than one way to answer it."

"What's the answer you feel like giving today, then?"

She snorts. "Would you believe me if I said I missed it?"

"I might, if you told me what you missed."

Gram stretches her legs out in front of her with a slight wince. She's zipped up in a jacket despite the heat, legs clad in stockings that make me sweat just looking at them. She stares out at the woods as she talks.

"Wasn't born here. Wasn't born far, mind you, just a hop, skip, and a jump some way, but I didn't grow up in Coldwater. This was Charlie's place. His home. The people, they was Charlie's, too. So, when our relationship took a turn for the worse, there wasn't nobody I could talk to. It was just me, all alone with my thoughts and feelings. And then, one day, there was this woman."

She points toward the tree line. "Just over there. Cried the first time I saw one and couldn't stop," she says. "I hadn't cried so much since I was a little girl. But that dead woman, she cried with me just as hard. It didn't make much sense. She wasn't flesh and blood, didn't have no tears to fall into the dirt, but she could feel. She could make *me* feel, just pulled out all those feelings I'd been shoving down deep so I could keep functioning."

She looks at me. "I was scared. But not of her. Of what my life had become, maybe. Of who I'd become. I was a wife and a mama, but I wasn't a person. Every day was a 'get through this' day, and the reward I got from that was just another day exactly like it. Deal with the house, deal with the kids, deal with Charlie. So, when I saw that woman—and kept on seeing her, or women like her—it was a reminder. I was somebody. And when I remembered that, I couldn't keep on hiding that somebody away."

"But what about Coldwater did you miss?" I ask. Nothing about it sounds good. Nothing about it sounds miss-able.

Gram exhales, heavy and long. "That feeling of being seen. I've only ever really felt seen by the dead, I guess." She meets my eyes, flickering hers back and forth between them with a frown. "Their eyes make you feel like you belong somewhere. You've made this place your home and they approve of it. But it's a trade-off. You're theirs. This place is yours." She laughs dryly. "Why would you ever wanna leave? And God help you, if you do.

"You think about leaving," she says, her voice a whisper as she stares up at a group of clouds directly overhead, the only ones in the whole sky, "and everything's beautiful all of the sudden. Grass greener than you've ever seen it, the breeze sweeter. Like the town itself is begging you not to leave it. The dead women try even harder to finagle their way into your head and nature's in on it."

I close my eyes for a second as a breeze whisks by. It's not hard to imagine the desperation of the dead. I've already felt it for myself, haven't I? Begging so insistent it hums. Chill so deep it aches.

I wonder if that's all it takes to make a ghost—longing for something hard enough, long enough. Maybe that's all it takes to make a human, too.

Or a photograph.

I can't help but think of the tintypes we studied in photography class, direct positives on thin sheets of metal. There's always a haunted quality to them. A timelessness. They were my favorites.

After all, pictures highlight whatever it is in a person bright enough to be captured in a still image. And whatever that is— the soul or the spirit or something else—echoes still have it. I don't think they could affect people as much if they didn't.

Suddenly, I want to capture that. Coldwater as it was—and as it is.

It has all the makings of a portrait series for my portfolio.

Life and Death in Small Town Maryland.

Or *Humanity Across Centuries*.

Or, you know. Something way less cheesy and dramatic.

The thought is the first one in the past few days that isn't painful, so I cling to it with all my strength. I'm already imagining the smooth, familiar feeling of the shutter button beneath my thumb and the impossibility of an echo framed by my lens.

Somewhere down the street a woman yells after her kid. The birds chirp to each other above us in a tree. Gram pushes herself up off the step with a wince. I tilt my head back farther to look at her. She smiles at me, bending until I feel her lips brush against my forehead. It's unfamiliar, we still barely know each other, but there's tenderness in it.

"I guess what I'm trying to say is that you ought to be careful," she murmurs.

TWENTY

Ghosts are, I'm realizing, the hardest things to capture on camera. Finding them is easy. They're in the front yard or by the woods or walking down the street, though none have gotten as close to me since the one by Dad's house.

Still, they're little more than blind spots to my camera.

A weird streak of sunlight. A glare. Once, a long motion blur. But there are no details. Nothing that captures their sad eyes; nothing that hints at the women they used to be.

Maybe it's because I'm too nervous to get close. A headache sparks every time I try and my hands grip my camera tight to keep from shaking. So, I keep my distance, use my telephoto lens, and hope that it works.

It never does.

Of course it doesn't because that's not how portraits work, ghosts or not. They're not taken in secret from ten feet away. They're taken up close, with connection and purpose.

I know that eventually I'll have to get closer. I *want* to get closer. But my first echo encounter is harder to shake off than I thought it would be.

Still, at least it keeps my attention off Mom. We've barely talked since her confession a week ago, and I don't know when I'll be ready to start. As it is, we've had other things to worry about. The doctors discovered new tumors in Gram. Now every trip to the hospital is full of numbers and words like *absolute neutrophil count* and *daptomycin* and *metastasis*. Doctors and nurses make up at least 60 percent of my daily human interaction.

Kat makes up the other 40 percent. When I'm not drinking free hot chocolate, we text constantly. She sends me memes I've already seen and links to Instagram profiles of cute dogs. She texts me selfies of her with her hair piled atop her head like a mop; her with no makeup; her with a pizza the size of an entire table.

There's a line between flirting and friendship, and I don't know which side we're on, but I'm not willing to question it. If this is what my summer's going to be—hospitals and tense car rides, failed photo after failed photo—then I can at least focus on the good parts without overthinking.

Or, well, *trying* not to overthink.

I text Leslie, too, of course, but she's actually out enjoying her summer. She responds fast, but a flurry of emojis is her go-to, and with her phone usually on a towel somewhere while she floats in the Atlantic, our FaceTimes have been few and far between. It's hard to begrudge her her last Jersey summer, but it's also hard not to imagine that this is what our friendship will look like once fall begins and school starts.

And then there's James.

Knowing he's still waiting for some kind of definitive answer makes my replies to his texts stiff. Then the guilt that follows makes me ignore him for hours at a time, the red notification bubbles like accusing eyes. Recently, he's moved on from words to pictures, the language he knows I work best in.

A bin full of stuff his mom bought for his dorm room that he's never going to use.

A picture of his new Howard soccer jersey.

A cup of Rita's water ice topped with the worst duo of flavors known to my taste buds, chocolate peanut butter and passion fruit.

Those are easier to respond to. I snap a picture of a crawl space kitten or the view of the moon from my window or, once, Gram, frowning at me from beneath a heap of blankets. And they make me feel better. Like we're friends again, without all the messiness.

My phone buzzes loudly in the hospital room and I pick it up before it can wake Gram. It's Kat, following up her pizza selfie with another, this time of her grinning wide at a slice gooey with cheese, and a text: *Lunch break?*

I bite my lip against a smile. It's been a few days since I've seen her in person for longer than it takes me to order a drink, and I *have* been eager to tell her about my plans for my portfolio.

I hesitate before responding.

Fine, but I expect top-tier pizza.

Her reply is immediate. *You know it's mid at best. But I'm told my company is pretty great.*

I ignore the warmth in my cheeks and shove my phone into my pocket, heading to Gram's bed to say bye. She smells like the hospital now that she's been here so often. But she also still smells like the hair grease she uses, like castor oil and honey. I smile, surprised at how quickly the scent has become familiar.

"Be back later," I promise.

Gram's eyes are unfocused when she looks at me. She smiles slightly before her eyes slide shut again.

I slip out of the room, ignoring Mom, and remind myself that there's a hospital full of people here to help. That I'll only be right downstairs if anything goes wrong.

Kat's easy to spot, and not just because she's the only person eating pizza in a coffee-splattered apron. I can't help it as I raise my camera from its strap on my shoulder. "Say cheese."

She grins around a mouthful of cheese and pepperoni. "Cheese!"

I snap the picture and take the seat across from her. I grab a slice when she pushes the box toward me and immediately take a bite so I'm not smiling at her like a dork.

She tells me about work and waiting to hear back from Hampton, about her brother and his latest girlfriend, some girl from Texas who's always baking something new every time Kat steps foot in the kitchen. She tells me a story about Will that makes me choke on my pizza. Then she makes me a frozen hot chocolate so disgusting that it takes another slice of pizza and an entire bottle of lemonade to rid my mouth of the taste.

I don't know how much time has passed. Her lunch break is probably long over, and the pizza is nearly gone, but she makes no move to head back behind the counter. Instead, the full weight of her attention rests on me. She motions toward my camera.

"How's your portfolio going? Think of a new idea yet?"

I brighten. This is part of what I came down here to talk to her about, after all.

"I have, actually."

"Well?"

I take a deep breath. "I want to focus on the echoes."

I try to explain why. The sad, alive eyes of the dead. The semi-southern gothic of their existence. The aching, electric connection of women and their pain across centuries—the way we reflect and amplify and exaggerate.

"I want to do a portrait series, I think. Echoes and Coldwater women. You know, put portraits of everyone side by side and see whether or not the echoes resemble the living. If there's anything in them recognizable as dead or in any of us that's recognizable as alive."

I pause, trying to untie the giant knot of this idea in my head.

"I want to keep it small. I don't want to go running around asking everyone if I can take their picture. Just a few echoes I see most often and the people in Coldwater I've come to know and lo—" I clear my throat quickly. "That I've gotten to know."

I turn to her, finally, both hands in my pockets to keep from fidgeting. "So, I wanted to ask if you'd be willing to be a part of it. If you wouldn't mind letting me photograph you."

"No."

I blink at Kat in surprise, but her usual grin is nowhere to be found. Instead, she's frowning, arms folded tight across her chest. I don't think I've ever seen her so still.

"No?" I repeat. I try to keep the weight of my disappointment out of my voice.

"No. Seeing them around is one thing, that's unavoidable. But what would you have to do to get a good picture of one? Follow it? Talk to it?"

"Maybe. It'd be easier to go to the schoolhouse, I think, and—"

Her frown deepens. "Are you stupid? You felt what they do to people for yourself, and you want to *go to the schoolhouse*? Where they *all* are?"

I stare at her, too surprised to be angry. "Don't talk to me like that."

"Then don't do stupid things like hang around women you can see through! Also. Also! Say you do take their pictures. Then what? Have you thought about what would happen if you started showing them to people? Yeah, sure, you might get into Parsons. Great. You know what else you might get? Stalkers. Fanatics. People around the world looking at you for answers. And I don't just mean paranormal investigators or the super religious. I mean scientists and people from the government. They would freak out. And they'd be right to. The point is, Jericka: They're dead. *That's* the difference between them and us. Just because they can mimic your feelings doesn't mean you should read deeper into that, or get attached, or take photos of them. Being around them changes people. They get in your head."

Exactly, I want to say. *That's exactly the point, that they're alive and conscious enough to do that.* Instead, I lean forward. "Being around *anyone* can change a person."

"Jericka—"

"I mean it. All personal ties affect people. How are the echoes any different? They were people before, they're people now, like we all are. That's the point of the portraits. That's the point of *photography*. And I think that would be the main focus if the pictures got beyond the admissions office, which they probably wouldn't. Everything you said is just an exaggeration."

"I don't think—"

"Besides, maybe what the echoes do is the only way they have left to communicate."

"Who cares what they're trying to say?" she snaps. "You can be as nice to them as you want! You can take their picture and try to talk to them, but do you really think they'll give a damn? If you want to leave this place even a little, that's it. You're the enemy. And all they want from you then is to change your mind."

I study Kat's face in silence. The scowl she fought to maintain is gone. Her eyes are far away as she glares down at the pizza box.

"What happened, Kat?" I ask as softly as I can. I've never seen her like this—angry and near tears.

She runs a hand over her face. "I was a kid with abandonment issues who'd grown up seeing echoes and realized they would never leave me. So, I made friends with them. I stopped hanging out with any of my actual friends, stopped doing things with the Waynes.

"Me and my dad got into a fight one day. My mom wanted me and Wayne to visit and I didn't want anything to do with her. So, I left. I figured I could stay in the schoolhouse, like spending the night at a friend's house." She grimaces. "I'm not gonna go into detail, but it was a mistake. When the Waynes found me, I was crying in a corner. I didn't stop crying for hours. I'd never felt that way before. Just . . . overwhelmed and drained. Like every good thing I recognized in myself had been taken."

She flashes me a grin that disappears just as quickly as it came. "Not sure I ever got all of it back."

My heart aches for her. "Kat . . ."

She laughs dryly, leaning back in her chair. "How's that for the childhood trauma I promised you, huh?"

"I didn't mean to—"

"I know you didn't. And I'm not your mom; you can do whatever you want for your portfolio. But I don't want to be involved. And like I said, it's a stupid idea."

"You don't have to come with me."

"You're going to get yourself hurt," she says. Sighing, she slumps against the table until her head is in her hands. She looks up at me through her lashes. "You don't know what you're doing."

That's true. I never do. Still.

Kat straightens up and stands, throwing out the napkins and finding a smaller container to put the leftover pizza into. I watch her in silence. The café is bigger than a hospital room, but it still feels too small for all the tension we've filled it with. I want to apologize, on instinct, but I don't think I've done anything wrong. I asked. She refused. We both have to move on.

When she turns back to me, her expression is carefully blank. No more anger. No more vulnerability. Not a hint of the playfulness I'm used to seeing in her. "I've gotta get back to work."

I nod. "Right. Sure."

I walk toward the door. Kat shared a big piece of herself with me, a big piece of her past, but I can't help feeling like I sacrificed some of her present self for it.

I turn around, ready to apologize for overstepping. But her back is to me as she fiddles with the coffee machine, and I can't find the words I want to get her to turn around.

TWENTY-ONE

By the end of June, we've all settled into a routine. Mom hangs out with Gloria on Mondays. Kat and I meet on Wednesdays at the diner to share a plate of cheese fries and a slice of apple pie. She doesn't ask me about my photo series and I don't offer up any information, so the air between us stays clear. Tuesdays and Thursdays are Gram's chemo days, and Mom and I switch off. On good days, Gram lets me stay with her. We quiz each other on old Hollywood stars and watch movies on my laptop. On bad days, I visit Kat at work or sit in the waiting room, texting Leslie.

I've been looking up new ways to capture the echoes on camera, too, scouring anything from ghost-hunting websites to articles about the best way to get clear shots of the sun. So far, nothing has worked. But the good thing about the internet is that it rarely runs out of information, even on the wildest things.

Today, though, is a deviation from the norm. It's the last day of summer school at Coldwater High, and me and Kat are on our way to campus for what Kat will only refer to as "tradition." She ignores all my guesses, smirking the entire way there.

"You'll see," is all she says, and when we pull into the parking lot, I definitely do.

Anyone under the age of twenty and over the age of twelve is here. They sit on the hoods of cars and huddled in the backs of pickup trucks, on the school stairs and even on blankets on the asphalt. The energy in the air is infectious and eager, and even though I don't know what we're waiting for, the excitement stirs in me, too.

"Okay," I say, taking her offered hand as I climb onto the roof of her car, "what's going on?"

The bell rings shrilly before she can answer and the fire alarm joins it a second later. The doors to the school burst open, and out pours a flood of students, cheering and throwing folders and papers into the air like it's graduation day. For some of them, maybe it is.

Everyone in the parking lot greets them with an earsplitting, unifying cheer. I join in, laughing as people take off down the street running side by side like they're in a track meet. A tall white boy wearing a baseball hat even hops on a horse tethered to a nearby pole, joining the race, and the screams grow louder.

"Seriously, what is this?" I yell over the screams and whoops.

Kat gives another loud cheer as someone does a backflip off the school steps before grinning at me. "Freedom Day. The high school doesn't have AC, so summer school might as well be a death sentence. When it's over, everyone gathers here and cheers on the kids who made it. Some people race around town hollering. We usually go get ice cream afterward." She laughs. "In groups, anyway. Alma would have a heart attack if we swarmed her shop all at once."

"How many people here go to summer school?"

She laughs. "Too many."

She slides halfway down her car before hopping up and offering me a hand. "C'mon," she says, "let's go find Mae and Will. The shop always runs out of peach first, and I'm not missing out this year."

We only find Mae. Will, it turns out, joined the runners. He meets up with us at Alma's ice cream shop, sweaty and panting and shoving the last of an ice cream cone into his mouth. He pulls Mae into a kiss with ice-cream-covered lips, and even though she punches him in the shoulder, it's the widest I've seen her smile yet.

When it's finally our turn in the shop, Kat's in luck. There are a handful of peach scoops left, enough for her to order a double. I order summer berry, which is full of strawberries, blueberries, and raspberries. And Mae gets toasted marshmallow with chocolate chunks. With our ice cream and a handful of extra napkins in tow, we find a noncrowded spot in a nearby park. Will perches, unsurprisingly, on top of a bench, stealing spoonfuls of Mae's ice cream below. Me and Kat sit cross-legged in the grass, enjoying the sun and the taste of summer fruit on our tongues.

Sitting here, it's so easy to imagine the life I could have

had if I'd stayed with Dad. The blueberries on my tongue taste tarter than normal as I swallow another spoonful.

"You have to taste this, Jericka," Kat says. "It's the only thing I'll miss when I leave this place."

"Um, we're right here!" Mae says, and Kat laughs.

"The only *food* I'll miss," she clarifies, scooping a spoonful and holding it out to me. "C'mon," she says. "Taste."

I hesitate. "You sure you don't want me to . . . ?" I hold up my own spoon and she shakes her head.

"No offense to summer berry, but I don't wanna mix flavors. I mean, if you're cool with it. I can grab another spoon."

"No, it's fine." And it's not a big deal, really. It's just sharing ice cream. Ice cream from Kat's spoon. A spoon that has been in her mouth.

I lean forward to taste the ice cream before it can melt. And it's great. Peachy and creamy and faintly salty.

"Good, right?"

I blink. When did our faces get so close? The warmth in Kat's eyes makes me flush, and I lean back so quick I almost fall over.

"Uh-huh," I agree. "Delicious."

◊

Uncle Miles is home for the first time since Mom and I arrived, so we're trying out dinner as a family. I've even managed to convince everyone to watch a movie with me afterward, with a promise that I'd wash the dishes and a reminder to Uncle Miles that we'd bought a pint of rum raisin for dessert.

For the first half of *Lilies of the Field*, things are fine. I share a couch with Gram, Mom takes the armchair, and Uncle Miles pulls up a chair from the kitchen. We watch Sidney Poitier try to convince a group of nuns to pay him for the work he does around their convent.

Then there's a loud noise. It's the wind or one of the pans shifting in the sink. Mom jumps and Uncle Miles stiffens, and when I look over at them, just for a second, they look terrified. I keep my eyes locked on Mom's face, so I notice the exact moment her fear drains away and something—shame, maybe embarrassment—replaces it. She swallows hard and rubs absently at her bad wrist.

"It was probably nothing," I assure them.

My mind is on Gram's story about their movie traditions as Uncle Miles looks over his shoulder. Even Gram is sitting up a little taller than she was. It's as if they're all expecting the ghost of my grandfather to come walking in. Considering everything I've seen in this town so far, I'm not altogether sure he won't.

"Time for an intermission," Uncle Miles suggests.

He stands, opening the nearest window even though the fan is on. Mom walks into the kitchen without a word, and I follow her. She moves like she's on autopilot. Finding and filling a kettle with water. Putting it on the stove to boil. Grabbing a mug from one of the cabinets.

She smiles at me with the corner of her mouth as she leans

heavily against the counter. "It's easy to get spooked in this house," is all she says.

We stand in silence until the kettle whistles and the noise pulls Mom out of her own memories.

"Whose pickup truck was that you pulled up in earlier?" she asks as we head back into the living room.

"Kat's brother's," I say. He'd borrowed her car for something, so she borrowed his to drop me off.

"Nice of her." Mom takes a sip of tea and her shoulders settle. "I'm glad you've made a friend." She studies my face carefully. "Is she just a friend? Gloria was telling me that Asia—"

"Would it matter?" We don't talk for more than a week and now she wants to question me about this?

"I think it might to James. How is he?"

"He's fine." He's also none of her business. Still, guilt gnaws at me anyway, the way I'm sure Mom meant for it to. "Kat is just a friend."

"I'm just making sure," she says, softening. "You don't need anyone trapping you here."

As if I don't have family here.

As if I'm not already aware of her feelings on this place.

"Who's her people?"

I laugh. I have never heard Mom ask that question, of anyone, in my life. Like the faint accent lingering behind her words, it must be a remembered thing. She notices, too, and wrinkles her nose at me.

"You talking about that Morris girl? Dwayne and Trish are her parents," Gram answers, breaking off her conversation with Uncle Miles. "They're about your age, maybe Miles's. You remember Dwayne's mama—she used to stop by here every so often with all her gossiping. I heard talk Trish ran off 'bout a decade ago, all in the middle-of-the-night like."

"Instead of in the middle of the afternoon while her kids were at school, like you?"

I tense. In the same way that we haven't talked much, neither have she and Gram. Three generations of not talking and not listening. Apparently, though, Mom's in the mood to talk tonight. History crackles like electricity in the room.

"I'm just saying," Mom continues, ignoring the warning look Uncle Miles shoots her. "We're in here watching a damn movie with her like we're kids again, but how many times did we walk around this town looking for her like we were playing some twisted game of hide-and-seek? How many beatings did it take until we learned to stop asking about her? To cry quieter when we missed her?"

Uncle Miles doesn't answer. He doesn't even look at her. Instead, he stares hard at the TV until she turns away to pin their mother with her gaze. Gram shakes her head, and if it's possible for her to look frailer than she did during her time in the hospital, she does now.

"Let her say what she wants. It's past due."

Mom's hands are shaking. Tea spills over the sides of her mug, dripping down her wrist. It must burn, but she doesn't seem to notice. She looks like an angry little girl, her eyes glassy with tears. "The leaving I can understand. But you left us with *him*. And you never came back."

Mom never talks about her dad. But it's not hard to imagine what he was like or the ways in which he hurt her and Uncle Miles. It's harder to imagine that, however bad he was, Gram wanted out enough to leave her kids behind like sacrifices to an angry god.

"No answer I give is going to change anything," Gram says after silence settles over the house. "The past is the past."

"That's it?" Uncle Miles's voice surprises me. He looks surprised, too, as if he hadn't meant to say it aloud. He keeps going, though. "Not even a sorry? Not even an 'if I could take it back, I would'?"

I don't want to breathe too loudly or be seen. This isn't something I should be part of. But Mom is hurting. Uncle Miles is hurting. If Gram can make it stop, she should.

She doesn't. She exhales sharply. "I'd go back if I could," she echoes. "But what good does that do for you now? Our lives have all been led. There's no unlivin' them. Me saying what you want to hear won't change that."

Gram pulls herself to her feet with a wince, leaning heavily against the arm of the couch. I move to help her, but she steadies herself and heads for her bedroom without looking at any of us. The door shuts firmly behind her.

Mom draws in a deep, deliberate breath. "I'm not doing this anymore."

TWENTY-TWO

"We can't just leave Uncle Miles alone," I try to convince Mom the next morning. She's busy emptying her closet and muttering curses under her breath. The drawers in her dresser are all off track and her suitcase is lolled open on her bed like a mouth awaiting food.

"He was doing fine before we got here," Mom points out.

"He wouldn't have called if he was. You wouldn't have come all the way out here if that was the case."

"Miles will be fine," she says sharply. "He's a grown man. He doesn't need my help with everything all the time."

"But Gram—"

Mom slams shut the drawer she's kneeling in front of and turns to me. "Listen to me. We don't owe this place anything." She takes my hand. "I came. I tried. But part of growing up is realizing you don't have to make yourself forgive people who hurt you. Especially when they won't even apologize."

I could point out the irony. The hypocrisy. But now doesn't feel like the time.

"What if she did?"

Mom doesn't even take a moment to think. The smile she gives is strained and sad. "Wouldn't matter. There are some wounds apologies can't heal." She turns back to her drawer, dropping my hand. She tosses a shirt toward the bed that misses by a few feet. "Go on, Jericka. Go pack."

"I don't want to." My voice is quiet. Uncertain. Mom keeps riffling through her drawer.

That's it, then. We're leaving. Again. A month ago, I might have jumped at the chance to go back to New Jersey, to beaches and familiar faces. But now I want to ride the summer out. I want to follow a stupid idea of photographing ghosts. I want to drink free hot chocolate in a hospital café with Kat and eat peach ice cream in the park. I want to talk to my dad again and beat Kya and Marcus in Mario Kart.

Coldwater isn't my home. But I've dug a place for myself in its red-brown dirt. If I leave now, it'll be so easy to get caught up in constant movement again. So easy to forget about the part of me that feels free out here. And I don't want to forget.

"I'm not going."

Mom barely spares me a glance. "Of course you are."

"You can't just take me again. I'm not some flower you can keep uprooting and planting over and over." I clench my jaw to steel myself. "I'm tired, Mom. Please. We can't just leave."

"I can leave," she says. It's almost like she needs to hear it said aloud. To remind herself.

"I can't."

How do I convince her that I can't continue this cycle? Gram leaves her leaves me leaves Gram. Maybe life is cyclical and growing up is just learning how not to be nauseous as everything spins around you.

"Gram is here now. She's here and so are you and maybe she won't apologize. But you haven't apologized to me, either. So, you should just talk."

Mom opens her mouth, and from the deep lines in her forehead, it's clear she means to argue. I cut her off before she can. "Aren't you tired of running away?"

Because I'm tired of being dragged along. I think of the echoes. I think of how stuck they are. I think I might give up a lot to be stuck somewhere.

"She's going to die, Jericka," Mom says softly. "Whether we leave or not. Staying here won't change anything."

Even as she says it, she starts picking up some of the clothes scattered on her floor. A pair of socks. A hot-pink pair of underwear. A shirt. She puts them in a drawer instead of her suitcase. "I'm not promising anything," she says.

◊

Now seems as good a time as any to take portraits of Mom and Gram, and not just because Mom could leave again at any minute. Gram's getting sicker. It's obvious. Her skin is a constant shade of gray brown, and the bags under her eyes have deepened despite the fact that she's asleep more often than not these days. She makes it through less and less of each movie we try to watch together, and she calls me Lacey sometimes, even if she usually catches herself right after.

The pictures are no problem, but getting them to talk is.

In the month or so that we've been here, there are a handful of things I can think of that Mom and Gram have talked about.

1.   Doctors' appointments
2.   Medicines
3.   Food
4.   Me
5.   Uncle Miles

That's it. Nothing else. I don't know if they're both too scared or just too angry, but whatever it is, it can't keep happening.

I won't let it.

Which is why we're all outside, beneath the thin shade of the porch, Mom in a chair dragged out from the kitchen, Gram in an old rocking chair. And me, standing in front of both of them with my camera in my hands.

"So, what're we supposed to be doing?" Gram asks. She's not actually rocking in her chair, just leaning heavily against the wood until it creaks. "You need us to pose or something?"

"I thought we were taking these separately," Mom says, frowning.

"Actually," I say, "I wanted to try a couple different things. Schools like variety in portfolios, you know?"

Before she can protest, I carefully take the photos out of my pocket. They're Gram's, the ones from her box. She'd shown a few to Uncle Miles last night and left them, forgotten on the table.

"I want to try and re-create some of these. Not exactly how they were, though. We'll take a few shots and see how it goes."

I'm playing things by ear, hoping I can at least get them sitting closer together. They both lean forward for a better look. In the first picture, Gram is smiling softly down at the round-cheeked baby version of Mom in her arms, holding a stuffed bear in her opposite hand.

Mom raises her eyebrows. "Don't think it's safe for either of us if I try to climb into her lap," she says dryly.

I resist the urge to roll my eyes. "That's why this is an interpretation, not an exact re-creation. Just . . . look at each other." I raise the camera to my face and add, "Like you love each other, I mean."

"I do love her," Gram says, turning slowly in her chair to face Mom. "Even if the feeling's not quite mutual."

Mom's more reluctant to turn. I gesture with a hand and, eventually, she does, too. "It's hard to love a stranger," she mutters.

They lock eyes. I watch them through my viewfinder.

There's so much tension in their faces. Faces that look surprisingly similar when they're set so close together. They have the same clench to their jaws, the same tilt of their heads.

Mom drums her fingers impatiently against the arm of her chair. Gram quietly taps her foot.

I snap a picture.

"Okay," I say, "what're you both thinking about?"

"About how long we have to do this."

"I'm thinking about everything I missed." I keep quiet, hoping that Gram might go on. She does. "Last I looked at you this close, you were in the fourth grade."

Mom yanks her head away. "Yeah, well, whose fault is that?"

Gram softens. "I've never denied that it's mine. But an old woman's allowed a little remembering. A bit of regret."

The breeze picks up, bringing pollen and the smell of freshly mowed grass. Mom whips her head back toward Gram as if it's pulled her along, too. "Oh, *now* you regret it?"

"I regretted it then, too. The minute I was gone." Gram sighs. "It wasn't what I meant to do. But plans change. They . . . fall apart. And I . . ." She squeezes both curved arms of the rocking chair until her knuckles are white. "I needed to go. Even if I'd stayed here, I wouldn't have been any good to you as a mama. Not as broken down as I felt myself getting."

Mom turns back to me. My camera is still up, I'm too nervous to put it down, to ruin whatever's happening here. My lens is zoomed in just enough to catch the shine of tears in her eyes. "Are we done here, Jericka?" she asks, ignoring Gram.

"Just, um. Just a couple more?"

She nods. I lower the camera and take out another picture. In it, both their backs are to the camera as they crouch in the grass. Their heads are leaned in close and Gram is pointing to something in front of them that the camera doesn't catch.

"Crouching's not a good idea," I say before Gram can stand. I step over to their right, stepping down off the porch. "Lean in close and look my way. A little closer, Mom."

When they're in position, I walk around to the other side of the porch so I'm behind them. Gram turns to face Mom. Mom keeps looking straight ahead.

"I should've come back," Gram says. "Long before your dad was gone, but certainly after, if only to show my face and tell you both that I loved you. Truth is, I was scared to death."

"Of what?"

"Plenty of things, but you and Miles hating me was a big one."

"We did hate you."

"Rightfully so. But I told myself that if I pictured you a certain way, then that's just how it was. If I imagined your daddy changed and you and your brother happy, that's what was happening. That was my reality. If I saw you and I saw on your faces how much you hated me, how much I'd let you both suffer . . ."

Gram brings a hand up to wipe away a tear.

"I was protecting myself and doing it at the risk of hurting you both. But you know what they say—outta sight, outta mind. I thought if I kept away, all the way away, no calls or nothing, you'd forget about me. I'd be a bad dream, maybe, or—"

"You were my mama," Mom says quietly, finally turning to

her as I quietly walk back around them. "And you left me with a monster. How could I forget that?"

The mask she tried to maintain is gone. Now her expression is wide open, her face scrunched up like she's holding back a sob. I don't think I've ever seen her look as heartbroken as she does now, and I'm not sure I want to. I shut my eyes behind the viewfinder.

"Didn't you love us?" Mom whispers.

I open my eyes in time to catch Gram nod. It doesn't help; if anything, Mom's expression crumples further. She lowers her head until her forehead's resting on Gram's shoulder. Hiding her face seems more important than keeping her distance right now. The shutter button is smooth beneath my thumb.

"Then why wasn't that enough?"

The insects and the birds all quiet down. The breeze stops. All of Coldwater holds its breath waiting for Gram's answer. It comes on a heavy sigh, like it's a question she's asked herself a dozen times and she always comes up short.

"I don't know. I could lie to you, baby, but that's really all I've got. I loved you both and it didn't stop me from leaving. I loved you both and it kept me from coming back."

TWENTY-THREE

My phone rings when I'm getting ready to go see a movie with Kat and her friends. It's a horror movie, something with lots of blood and an all-female cast that I've heard a lot about online. I'm not a huge horror fan, so I'm trying to think of the best way to react to jump scares that won't involve screaming.

I think that's why I don't notice James's contact photo when I answer.

"Hey, I'm almost ready. I just have to—"

"Where are you going?"

I blink. "James?"

He laughs. "Hi. Were you expecting someone else?"

"No! I mean, yes." I make a face at myself in the mirror before turning away. "I'm going out with friends soon and I thought you were one of them."

I'm careful to include the plural and I don't know why. It's the truth, after all, there will be plenty of other people with us.

But would it matter if there weren't? James isn't the jealous type.

Besides, there's nothing to be jealous of. I'm going out with friends.

I roll my eyes at myself.

"Glad to hear you made some friends." I can hear the smile in his voice. "Sounds like the summer's going better than you thought it would."

I sigh, sinking down onto my bed. "Yes and no." I change the subject before he can ask a follow-up. "I'm surprised you called."

"I know you wanted some time to think and that's not what I'm calling about," he adds quickly. "The fair's in town, and, you know, we usually go, so it made me think of you. It sounds like an excuse, I know. And I swear it's only half of one."

"What's the other half?"

"That's easy. I miss you."

"Oh." I hesitate before I respond, but the words come out easy. "I miss you, too."

And I do. I keep making myself forget about all my favorite parts of him, as if it will help make my decision any easier. My decision, which I have managed not to think about for a whole month now.

"Absence makes the heart grow fonder, huh?" He laughs. It's his self-conscious laugh, the one he gets whenever his parents brag about his soccer scholarship or a teacher praises his work in class. He's nervous, I realize. Somehow that calms my own nerves. I smile.

"My heart's always fond of you, James." Before either of us can ruin things by talking about how our hearts feel about long distance, I change the subject. Sort of.

"I got your text the other day—your mom is determined to fill up your entire basement with things she's buying you for school. She knows you can only bring so much, right?"

He chuckles. "Probably not, but me and my dad aren't about to be the ones to tell her."

But then my phone vibrates and I peek at the screen; it's almost time for the movie, and Kat's texted to let me know she's in my driveway.

"I have to get ready to go," I say, feeling guilty saying goodbye. "My movie's starting soon."

"What movie?"

"*No Man's Land.*"

"I hear that's good, but are your friends prepared for you to scream like a baby?"

"I won't!" He's pointedly quiet, and I groan. "I don't scream," I say again. "I just . . . squeal a little."

He laughs, and even I'm having a hard time suppressing my smile. "Fine," he says finally. "Let's test it when you get back. You, me, the original *Friday the 13th*. Loser pays for dinner."

I roll my eyes, scrunching the ends of my hair with gel that smells too much like rose and not enough like argan oil. "Deal," I agree. "But loser picks the place."

"Already preparing for your loss?"

I snort. "No, but a girl's gotta save up to pay for college, and you'll already be on a college budget."

My smile fades when I realize we're making plans. Not quite for fall, but close enough to it.

"I really have to go," I say again, softer.

He picks up on my change in tone. Of course he does.

"Everything okay?"

I force a smile so he'll hear it in my voice. The mirror reflects it back at me, my face false and foreign. "Of course. Just trying to think of how I'll tell my new friends what a wimp I am apparently."

"It'll be good practice for our bet," he says. "It was good to talk to you, Jer; I really do miss you. Have fun."

◊

The bubble gum stench of Kat's car hits me harder than it usually does when I slide into the passenger seat.

"Did you get a new air freshener?" I ask. "I hate it."

She laughs. "Hi to you, too."

I grimace. "Sorry. Hi."

I roll down my window as she reverses out of the driveway, turning toward the breeze. I catch her glance at me.

"You good? It's really not a new air freshener, but we can catch a ride with Mae and Will if you hate it that much."

"No, it's fine. Really." Guilt piles on top of existing guilt. "I guess I'm just not feeling great."

"I'm not sure seeing a crap ton of fake blood will fix that. You're sure you want to come? We can do something else."

I try to ignore the way my heart leaps when she says *we*, or the fact that she's willing to abandon her plans to hang out with me. I ignore her question, too. "Can I ask you something?"

"Course."

"Why are you into horror movies if you hate the real-life ghosts in Coldwater?"

Kat tenses, but only for a second. "Murderers on-screen will probably give me nightmares, at worst. Echoes here like to cause irreparable emotional damage. One's way less fun than the other. And a lot less fake."

"Yeah, but." I straighten up in my seat, twisting toward her. "Scared is scared, right? If you can get over it for a movie, you could probably get over it in real life."

Stop it, Jericka. I'm poking the bear, as Mom likes to say, but I can't help myself. Kat and I are too close. I know it. I've known it for a while. But it's been so easy to rationalize.

We're friends, I assure Mom.

Friends, I tell James.

Friends? everyone in Coldwater questions, with their hawkish stares and carefully pursed lips.

But when I'm with her, laughing at something she says or admiring the shade of her lipstick that's always somehow perfectly suited to her skin, it's not as easy to believe. Being around her makes me feel . . . untethered. Like I'm a hot-air balloon and she's unwound the rope keeping me grounded. Everything's still there—all my worry and anxiety and fear. It'll be waiting for me when I come down. But when I'm with Kat, it's so far away that it barely matters.

It's not fair to James, who I've just promised a date with when I get home, who is so good at keeping me grounded in the best way possible.

And it's not fair to Kat, who looks at me sometimes in a way that's not friendly at all.

So, I need to end this, whatever this is.

The quickest way I know how.

"I mean, they didn't hurt you, right?" I continue. "They can't actually touch you. I know you think it's stupid for me to try and get closer to them, but I don't know. I think it's stupid to be as afraid of them as you are."

Kat, for her part, is good at keeping her cool. She keeps her voice light even as her grip on the wheel tightens. "Well, you know. We all have our flaws."

"Are you worried your obsession with them is going to keep you here? I mean, it already made you depressed, right?" I grip the side of the seat. "What if you don't get into Hampton? What if you're just stuck he—"

"Don't."

"Don't what?"

"Don't be an asshole out of nowhere. If something's wrong, then say that. You're not a baby, Jericka; you can use your words."

"Maybe I just don't want to do this anymore."

She glances at me. "Do what?"

"I don't know!"

Between things with her and James and my portfolio and Gram and what will happen when I go back to New Jersey, I'm scared of what will come crashing down on me all at once. There are too many unknowns. Better to take this one thing off the table now and save my future self the trouble.

The car slows to a stop on the side of the road. We're not far from my house, which still means we could be anywhere in Coldwater. Kat puts the car in park and turns to me with a frown.

"What's your problem?"

I can't help my scowl. "I already told you I don't know."

"Well, figure it out quick." She looks away, eyes darting between the windshield and every window. "You know how the echoes get. The last thing we need is them sensing you and—"

"The echoes!" I scoff. "Who cares! Are you going to let them control how you feel forever?"

Kat grits her teeth but she doesn't yell back. "No, but I don't feel like getting swarmed because you randomly decided you wanted to pick a fight. You want to take pictures like they're pretty little mysteries, go ahead. I won't stop you. But you don't get to act like I'm crazy when you've felt them, too."

I glare at her, heart thundering in my chest.

I don't actually want to hurt her feelings. I just want to understand my own better, to know why I don't light up thinking about James the same way I do when I think about Kat.

Kat, who I've known for a month.

Kat, who's staring at me like she has no clue who I am.

I'm sorry.

"I don't want to go to the movie," I say instead.

My head is throbbing. I shut my eyes and the colors behind my eyelids—orange and red and black—throb, too.

"I want to go home." I can feel her eyes on me even before I open mine. She reaches for the gear shift without a word, but I stop her. "I'll walk."

I get out before either of us can say anything else and start walking as quickly as I can.

I glance back, just once. Her car hasn't moved. It's not until I'm nearly a mile away that I see it pulling off.

Eventually, I pause.

Wait for a familiar pressure, that foreign intrusion that comes with an approaching echo. If I'm out here, already feeling a mess, I might as well try and be productive about it. I've only got my phone, but it's not like the camera has been much help; maybe it'll work.

I turn the flashlight on low and squint into the dark.

There's nothing and no one.

If there are any echoes out tonight, they're either far away or not focused on me. Maybe even they can't be bothered to try and unravel everything I'm feeling.

I start walking again, but I keep the flashlight on, following the thin arc of light home.

◊

A few days later, Asia and I stare at each other from opposite sides of her room. After a second, she gestures toward a circular plush chair in the corner and goes back to flipping through a magazine.

"So," she says, "not joined at the hip with our resident ghost girl anymore?"

She glances up with raised eyebrows and a smirk when I don't say anything. "I was kidding, but maybe there really is trouble in paradise. What happened, she trade you for a ghost?"

I glare at her. "You know we don't have to talk, right? We can just sit here in silence until I leave."

Which is hopefully sooner rather than later. Considering how loudly Mom and Gloria are laughing downstairs, I'm not counting on it. Mom barely listened to any of my protests when she dragged me out the house, my first time outside since my fight with Kat, marching me straight to the car.

"You need to talk to more kids your age," she said, as if Gloria wasn't the only person in the entire town besides Uncle Miles that she talked to. As if I don't—didn't—hang out with Kat all the time. "I'm sure Asia would love to get to know you better."

"Yeah, but where's the fun in that?" Asia says now, uncrossing her legs and stretching across her bed until she's facing me. Her smirk only grows. "If I guess what happened, will you tell me?"

"No."

"So, something *did* happen."

I sigh. I'm not in the mood for this. "Why do you care? Why do you hate her so much?" I'm reminded of something Kat said. "Is it because of your crush on her brother?"

"What?" Asia laughs so loud and hard it squeaks at the end. "Is that what she said?"

I shrug and she rolls her eyes.

"I don't hate her. I just think she gets a lot of unnecessary attention, what between her mom leaving and her ghost thing and her being a lesbian."

"So, you're jealous."

Asia narrows her eyes. "No. But for someone so quick to talk shit about this town, she sure holds a lot of its attention."

I don't know if Kat would agree, but I can see where Asia's coming from. Kat knows a lot of people, and it feels like she's friends with even more. It's obvious when we're in town together. Part of it is probably her jobs, but another part is her personality. You can't help but like her. I ignore the twinge in my chest.

"You're upset that she's popular."

"I'm *upset* that she acts like everyone in Coldwater is a brain-washed asshole if they like it here or if they're not constantly complaining." She rolls onto her back. "Sure, it's small. And bor-ing. And everyone is nosy." Her eyes flicker my way, though I'm not sure if she can actually see me. "But it's home, you know? And I love it."

"I think you're the first person I've met that actually loves being here."

She snorts. "Not a surprise. Like I said, you and Kat have been joined at the hip this whole time."

I can't resist the urge to snark. "Yeah, well, now we're not."

Asia sits up to look at me with a genuine smile. "Come with me to the river party this weekend, then. Meet new people. People who actually *like* Coldwater."

I can't help thinking of the last party Asia took me to.

"Thanks. But I think I'm all partied out."

"You take pictures, right?" I nod, uncertain. "Then come for the pictures, at least. Town is boring, but river parties aren't. Everyone's more themselves in the dark, after all. C'mon. What else would you be doing, anyway?"

Feeling sorry for myself in the attic of my dying grandmother's house, probably. Chasing ghosts, maybe.

Definitely trying not to think about James or Kat.

"No" sits squarely on my tongue. But it's "Okay" that comes out instead, surprising us both.

TWENTY-FOUR

The river is murky, somewhere between green and brown. A few ropes are tied to the branches of nearby trees, and people swing into the water, shouting before they vanish beneath the surface. There aren't too many people in the river. Most lounge on the bank. There are beer cans and plastic cups in everyone's hands, and loud music shakes the leaves overhead.

It doesn't look too wild, but the sun's still out.

I follow Asia toward a group of people camped out close to the river on a patchwork of blankets and towels. My eyes sweep over the water. It takes a second before I realize I'm looking for Kat. I quickly turn my attention to my camera instead, making sure my settings are right for low light.

"I know the photo angle was my way of convincing you to come, but that's not the only thing you're planning to do, is it?" Asia asks, eyeing me from across the blanket we've settled on. She takes off her shirt before I can respond, revealing the gold bikini top underneath. "You at least brought a bathing suit, didn't you?"

I didn't. "I'm just gonna take a couple test shots," I say, getting up, careful to keep my back to the water as someone nearby does a cannonball. "I'll be right back."

Asia doesn't try to stop me as I slip away into the woods. Someone's brought a few folding tables and shoved them between two half-fallen trees. A lid-covered punch bowl sits on top surrounded by cling-wrapped plates full of cookies and chips. Someone more responsible than the rest has even brought a fruit salad.

I raise my camera to my face, adjusting the lens to see how close a shot I can get of the river from here. There's a giant moth on a tree a few feet away, flapping its wings lethargically, and a couple making out too close to poison ivy. There's a rotting log and a pair of abandoned swim trunks and . . . one really pissed-off Mae.

Somehow in the second it takes me to lower my camera and actually look at her, her scowl deepens.

"What are you doing here?"

"I was invited?"

Her lips tighten as she looks me over. I'm not much to look at. The sundress I'm wearing is old, the floral pattern faded, and my camera strap is bulky and black around my neck. She's wearing a black-and-white striped bikini top, her stomach bare except for a dangling belly button clip, and shorts. She looks good. I don't think she'd appreciate it if I told her so.

"Look, I'm done playing nice," she says abruptly. I want

to ask when she started, but I keep my mouth shut. "I don't know what you were playing at with Kat, but she's not a toy. If you're here for some summer fling while you're away from your boyfriend or whatever—"

"I'm here because my grandmother is *dying*," I interrupt.

"I don't care," she snaps, harshly enough that I flinch. "I care about Kat and keeping her from getting her feelings hurt by people who stay just long enough for her to get attached."

"I'm not—"

"You're not what? Going to leave? Going to hurt her feelings? From what I hear, you've already done one of the two."

"I'm not going to bother her anymore," I say softly.

Mae sizes me up in quick, sharp glances. Everything about her is ripe with protectiveness. I could almost appreciate her being such a good friend if she didn't also scare me a little. Eventually she snorts, tossing her head in disgust. "You're both liars."

I blink. "What?"

"Kat said the same thing, and she looked just as hard to believe."

She's already walking away before I can say anything else, bare feet leaving imprints in the wet soil. "If you hurt her again," she calls over her shoulder, "I'll drown you in this river."

I bring my camera up to take a picture of her retreating form against the water. I don't doubt her.

◊

Sunlight fades all at once, and when it does, the party shifts into a higher gear. The music gets louder. Clothes come off. The excitement is bright enough to dim my anxiety and lingering guilt. Or maybe that's the alcohol. I'm halfway through my third cup of whatever Asia grabbed from the drinks table, and the night's starting to feel a little floaty.

Two people are making out in the sand while a couple of guys do backflips for a crowd of giggling girls cheering them on a few feet away. A bonfire's sparked up by a fallen tree on the shore. People gather around its warmth, watching the newborn flames quickly mature. I spy everything from my perch on a tree branch jutting out over the water, feeling a bit like a nosy owl.

"I thought parties weren't your thing."

I startle, blinking rapidly.

Kat emerges from the dark water like an apparition. She's in a maroon one piece that suits her dark skin. Her braids are up in a waterlogged bun that wobbles with her every movement. Water drips from her. Glistening on her cheeks, pooled in the dips of her collarbone.

God, she's gorgeous.

I look away from the rest of her to meet her eyes. "Sometimes," I say. "If I have the right company."

She nods behind me, where Asia, on the drunk side of tipsy, is talking loudly with her friends. "That's the right company?"

I sigh. "Not exactly. But it's who I came with."

Kat makes a noise of acknowledgment. "So, I think we need to talk, but I'm also freezing. Can we have this conversation in the water?"

The river is a slick of oil reflecting moonlight. It doesn't look like something I want to take my chances in. But there are dozens of other people still diving from ropes and stacked on each other's shoulders, playing chicken.

"You actually want to talk to me?"

"I came over here, didn't I?"

Instead of waiting for my response, she walks back into the water, sinking until only her face is visible. She lurks in the middle of the river like a siren, eyebrows raised. And I, like a fool eager to be lured to my death, hop down into the water beside her. She wrinkles her nose when I splash her. "You didn't bring a bathing suit?" she asks, glancing at the skirt of my sundress floating around me.

I doggy-paddle my way over to her until we're treading water side by side. "I was mostly here to take pictures and people watch."

"You know . . ." She grins. "Underwear is practically a bikini."

My heart thumps harder, faster. "Is that your way of trying to get me out of my clothes?"

Her grin widens. It could rival moonlight. "Could be."

My cheeks warm and I look away. Things feel tantalizingly easy between us again, like the other day in the car was some horrible dream. But it wasn't.

And it's my fault.

"I'm really sorry," I say. "I wish I could say I didn't mean to be such a jerk, but I did. I thought if I hurt your feelings, you'd never want to talk to me again and this . . . this whole thing would be easier. But I should have just told you how I feel."

Somehow, we're farther out than I remember us being a second ago. My feet no longer touch the bottom. The water feels warmer, and I try not to imagine everything that could be hiding beneath its murkiness. I glance at her in the silence that falls, but Kat's not looking at me. She's on her back, staring up at the sky.

"You'll give yourself a cramp treading water all night," is all she says.

I don't flip onto my back as gracefully as I want to. There's a bit of flailing and a jolt of panic, but she grabs my hand before I start to sink and my body relaxes enough to float. Water laps around my ears and covers my scalp. It's almost frightening how calm I feel and how instantly I feel it.

The noise of the party fades to the background.

"It wasn't what you said," Kat says finally. "Okay, it was. It was mean and unnecessary. But it was mostly the fact that it came out of nowhere. It didn't seem like you were angry, and I don't think I did anything wrong. I realized that maybe you were actually a completely different person than the one I thought I was getting to know."

I look over at Kat, hoping to catch the expression on her face. But most of what I see is her profile. She's staring straight up at the stars like she's telling them a story. "I felt like I was a bad taste in your mouth and you'd finally decided to spit me out."

My chest tightens, my throat with it. "It wasn't about you," I whisper.

"Yeah, I get that. But you made me feel like it was, and that was a shitty thing to do, Jericka."

"I know."

"Tell me, then."

"What?"

"You said you should've told me how you felt. So, tell me."

I lose my balance and quickly find my way back to the surface, coughing up the water that suddenly fills my mouth, my nose, my ears. I clumsily go back to treading water to give my body something to do while my heart beats a hundred miles a minute.

"I shouldn't," I say, when I can finally breathe again.

Kat snorts. "You shouldn't have been a jerk, either, but here we are."

Sometime between me going under and popping back up again, she transitioned into treading water, too. Now we stare at each other, feet rippling the water around us, moon like a spotlight.

If I'm going to admit how I feel about her, it should be now. *To* her. No more hiding behind a fifty-foot friendship wall.

Okay.

This is fine.

"Kat, I . . ."

This is fine, this is fine, this is fine.

I can feel my throat closing, my breath coming too quick. I

can do this. I'm not going to have a panic attack in the middle of the water because I can't tell a girl that I like her.

"I . . ."

SPLASH!

A boy with dark curls pops up between me and Kat with a holler. "Ay, yo, Matt! I told you I could swing farther than you! Now how 'bout you . . ."

He trails off as he swims away from us without a word of apology. Kat and I stare at each other in shock and burst out laughing. While not all the tension is gone, the surprise cannonball shattered a good deal of it.

Kat shakes her head, still laughing. "C'mon," she says. "Let's get a drink and talk on land before one of these jackasses lands on *us* next time."

TWENTY-FIVE

My dress is still dripping from my impromptu swim, but the breeze is warm and I'm drying quickly. Kat knows so many people that it takes us half a dozen polite smiles and quick chats to reach the drinks table.

I'm almost pulled into a conversation between two people heading to New York for college before Kat grabs my hand and leads me away.

They're nothing special on their own, my hands. But in hers they're some kind of magic. I flex, testing out the fingers I've had my entire life like they're something new, and her hand tightens reassuringly in mine. I've lost count of how many drinks I've had, but there's a pleasant feeling coursing through my veins that makes everything shimmer. When I take a sip of my latest, Kat watches me over the rim of her own with her usual grin.

"What?" I ask.

"You like me."

"What?"

"That's what you were going to say, wasn't it? That's why you were being such a jerk." She laughs, hard enough that she has to set her cup down. "Oh my God. Were you doing the girl version of 'he's mean to you because he likes you'?"

I stare at her, spluttering for a good five seconds. "I . . . what . . . no! *No!*" I mean, sort of. But also, absolutely not? "That's *not*—"

But Kat is laughing too hard to listen to whatever I'm trying to say. She's near tears at this point. "You were!" She grips the edge of the table to keep herself upright and grins at me like she's about to burst into more laughter at any moment. "I'm not even mad anymore. I'm really not."

I groan, burying my face in one hand. "It's really not like that."

"Please," she says, taking another sip of her drink, nearly choking when she starts laughing again, "explain."

"I'm not explaining anything while you look so smug."

She bats her eyelashes at me. "I don't know what you're talking about. This is how I always look."

I roll my eyes, and when she grins, I can't help but return it. I take a sip of my quickly warming drink. When I lower my cup, I catch her eyes flicker down toward my lips. I glance away. Take another sip. My entire mouth is suddenly dry.

The lightness between us shifts into something new. It lingers on my skin like water from the river. I speak before I get too caught up in it.

"I really am sorry, Kat."

She smiles. "I believe you." She pauses, then adds, "And I really do forgive you." She nudges me, pressing her shoulder briefly to mine. "Everyone gets an asshole pass now and then."

I smile, but it fades when she turns to grab a cookie. My apology might have solved one problem I created for myself, but the others remain.

My feelings for Kat.

My inability to take any sort of next step with James.

My guilt over both.

Not to mention the nonexistent portfolio that my college application relies on.

I down the rest of my drink, shuddering at the aftertaste. "Kat?"

She turns to me, eyebrows raised, an oatmeal raisin cookie between her teeth. The sight is so silly, so her, that it makes things easier. "I like you."

The world doesn't end. I don't get an angry phone call from a heartbroken James.

Kat stares at me for a second before she takes the cookie out of her mouth. "C'mon," she says. "I want to show you something."

"Where are we going?" I ask, following her away from the party and the river, half stumbling over roots.

"There's this place," Kat says, and her voice whips into me as we run. "It's like a lightning bug world."

When we stop, we're in a field. I couldn't tell it from any other field if you paid me, but she's right. It's fantastic.

There are hundreds of thousands of stars in the sky, and

it looks like a few dozen have fallen to earth. It takes me a moment to realize that they haven't. That these are the lightning bugs she was talking about. They move in unison, flitting this way and that, forming circles of light around each other and around me and Kat. It's the most magical thing I've ever seen.

Beyond them is real night. Even with the stars and the lightning bugs glowing their brightest, a person could lose themselves in this darkness.

We lie down, facing the sky.

"I like you, too," Kat says after a while.

I turn to look at her. Her face is so close to mine. Her eyes are all golden irises and long, wispy lashes. She has the kind of eyelashes you make wishes on. She reaches out a hand and a lightning bug settles into it like it was called. It's strange up close. Its eyes are huge and its long black bottom flickers with warm light, illuminating the inside of Kat's palm.

"You think it can actually see us?" she asks. "Or are we just shadows to it? Echoes, maybe."

"I don't know," I admit.

Crickets converse nearby, and the wind picks up, rustling the trees overhead. There's something different about lying next to her in the grass now. When we slipped away at her party, there was something furtive about it but still unfamiliar, like making eye contact with a stranger on a train. A brief connection before you both go back to your own lives.

This feels like a step further. Like whatever happens in this clearing tonight will be life-defining.

I let out a breath. "What would you do if you were a bird?" I ask. The question startles a laugh out of her.

"A bird?" she repeats. "Why a bird?"

It was the quickest thought, easy enough to grab on to. Something besides our mutual crush. I shrug.

"What kind of bird?"

"Any kind."

Kat thinks a moment. Actually thinks, I know, because her teeth find her bottom lip.

"I'd shit on people's heads," she says eventually. "And their cars."

I laugh. "A bird of chaotic evil."

"That's just all birds. What about you? What would you do?"

"Make a nest."

"That's all?"

"It just seems like it would be nice," I say, "to make a home for yourself. Something permanent."

Her hand grazes mine and I let it. I feel her closeness with every breath, and when she turns to me, her eyes are bright. Searching.

My thoughts are incoherent but urging. They move my face closer to hers. My lips closer to hers. My pulse thrums wildly. My entire body burns.

"I like you," she says again.

"I—" I say.

It's all I say. We're kissing, suddenly—*not suddenly*—and I'm not sure who kissed who but I don't care. Her lips are on mine and *God*, they're soft. My thoughts still to nothing. There is only the two of us, aglow in a quietly humming field of lightning bugs.

Kat kisses like she smiles. Like she laughs. Fully and wonderfully. I want to bottle her soul like a lightning bug, watch it glow through the glass. Let it fill me with some inexplicable lightness like maybe I'm capable of glowing, too. She leans into my palm splayed across her cheek, and the hand on the back of her neck tightens as I pull her closer to me.

Our kiss deepens and Kat's hands move. From cheek to throat to shoulder, following some sort of secret path. Her thumbs press into my hips, burning, chasing away the cool night. Her breath is just as warm against my neck. My breath hitches.

"Kat," I say. Or try to say. The circular motion of her thumb against my skin robs me of my voice.

"Hmm?" The word is little more than a hum against my neck as she nuzzles into me. I'm aware of her every breath. I haven't been as in touch with anyone since . . .

James.

"I have a boyfriend," I remind her. James's existence should be a shock of cold water, but Kat's fingers are still on my skin and my body is still on fire.

"Do you want me to stop?"

Of course I do. Wasn't it only a few days ago that I made plans with James?

Of course I don't. I don't ever want to stop kissing Kat.

But this isn't fair. Not to James, who's still waiting for

me. Not to Kat, who will still be here after I leave. Not even to me.

I don't reply, so she leans back. Sits up. The part of me that sighs in relief is tiny compared to how loudly my disappointment groans. I sit up, too.

"I'm sorry," I say, but she only smiles, resting her forehead against my shoulder. It's such a casual, comfortable thing. My heart shows no signs of slowing down.

"Don't be. I'm a little tipsy, for one."

"And two?"

Kat lifts her head. Her smile softens. "You've got some shit to figure out, don't you?"

TWENTY-SIX

A clap of thunder wakes me in the morning.

The sound echoes loudly in my head, quickly followed by a strike of lightning to the brain. I freeze in the middle of sitting up, hoping the pain will fade if I wait it out. It doesn't. Instead, it turns into a deep throbbing like my subconscious has learned to play the drums.

I run my hands over my face, gritting my teeth. There's no way I'm ever drinking again.

There's no way I'm leaving this bed.

Another boom of thunder. A few seconds later, the room is lit with lightning. Rain spatters against the window. Somewhere in the tangle of sheets, my phone buzzes. I reach for it, squinting at the screen. Mom.

Come downstairs.

Damn. Did she hear me come in last night? Did she decide to wait until morning to yell at me while I have a hangover like some sort of ultimate punishment? Or has she made up her mind and we're leaving?

My heart sinks. I bury my face in a pillow and groan. I text back, *Coming*.

I reach for my camera, groping around first on the bed and then the floor. I find it eventually, sticking halfway beneath the bed, and pull it toward me by its strap. I want to see the pictures I took last night, to remind myself that all of it was real. But when I press the power button, it doesn't turn on. I press harder. Still nothing.

"C'mon," I mutter, shaking it a little. "Please."

I check the battery light, but it isn't blinking, so it's not dead. My head throbs. I don't think it got wet. I'm pretty sure I kept it as far from the river as I could. But I wasn't exactly on my best behavior, and neither was Asia when I entrusted her with it. With a muttered prayer, I slip the memory card out and set it on the nightstand for safekeeping.

I'll deal with it later, when I'm more awake and less hungover.

By the time I manage to drag myself out of bed, my headache only goes from bad to worse. Still, I try to look as normal as possible before I head downstairs, slipping into the bathroom to wash my face and brush my teeth. The smell of bacon and syrup greets me when I open the bathroom door and guides me into the kitchen.

"It smells—" I say, and stop.

Either my guilt has manifested into a life-size, eerily

realistic version of James or he's actually eating bacon in Gram's kitchen. Considering the way Mom is grinning at me and how Gram is side-eyeing him, it has to be the latter.

James is here.

James is *here*.

It takes a minute to find my voice and another to make sure it doesn't waver. "What are you doing here?"

I wince. It comes out too harsh, like I'm accusing him of something. I try again, hoping I sound more pleasantly surprised. "You didn't tell me you were coming."

He wipes the grease from his hands and stands, enveloping me in a hug that I'm too shocked to return.

"It was supposed to be a surprise," he says into my hair.

"Consider me surprised," I mutter. Surprised and guilty and about two seconds away from throwing up. I step back quickly and his smile turns apologetic.

"Hopefully a good one. Your mom thought you might—"

"My mom?"

"She invited me. Said she thought you might like a familiar face from home."

A familiar face could have just as easily been Leslie's. Why James? Irritation and suspicion make my head throb more.

I glance over at her. She's standing at the stove, her back to me, but it's obvious that she's listening. "Yeah, well, I'm sure she's thrilled you're here." I don't bother hiding the sarcasm in my voice, but I regret it when I catch his smile slip. "Sorry. Mornings. You know how I am."

It's no explanation at all, really, but it seems to placate

him. It's funny how little you can get away with saying to a person when they know you well enough.

"Give me a second?" I ask, and he nods, reclaiming his spot next to Gram, who raises her eyebrows at me before pulling him into conversation.

I grab a glass and move toward the sink to fill it up, close enough to Mom that we can talk without being overheard. "Why did you invite him here?"

She arches an eyebrow at me, never taking her eyes off the bacon sizzling in the pan. "Why didn't you?"

"Because we're figuring things out right now and we both agreed that meant we needed a break."

"You *both* agreed? From the way he reacted when I invited him, it didn't sound like the case to me."

"Maybe if you had asked *me*, it would have." I stare at her. "I know you like James, but you didn't even invite him over when we were in the same state. Why now?"

Mom finally turns to face me. "Because lately it seems like you need reminding that life, and people, exist outside of Coldwater. We're here for the *summer*. That's it. No need to go changing your plans based on one girl and a couple of months."

I know this is more about Coldwater and less about me and Kat. But even if this whole summer is a wrong turn for her, a dead end, it's a whole new road for me.

"It's like you said: They're *my* plans. I'm allowed to change them if I want to."

I head over to the table before she can get mad about me catching an attitude.

James and Gram are still chatting. He's won her over clearly. Her stare has softened and there's a slight smile on her face while he talks, like she's indulging a favorite grandchild.

"Mind if I steal James for a second, Gram?" I ask.

She snorts. "Soon as he finishes up his story. You go on and make yourself presentable. Boy came all this way—least you can do is look nice."

I groan. Me looking my worst when people arrive for surprise visits is almost tradition at this point.

James smiles. "I always think Jericka looks nice."

Both Mom and Gram laugh, the same loud burst of amusement. Gram reaches across the table to pat James's hand. "Smart boy," she says. "But I know you got eyes in that head of yours."

◊

Apparently, it's the Fourth of July in Coldwater. Despite the earlier thunderstorm and the off-and-on-again rain, there are plans to celebrate. Mom tells me this when she drags me and James to the Food Lion. Well, she drags me. James comes along willingly.

"It's technically a Juneteenth party," Mom says. "But it's easier to get fireworks closer to the Fourth."

She starts to grab a cart, but James beats her there, waving her off as she goes to push it. Mom smiles. "It's usually a few of us—Coldwater, Spring Grove, Sharptown, sometimes. And it's almost always on the second." Mom frowns as she steps around a huge puddle of water. "Rain or shine."

While she scours the store's crowded aisles, James and I fall a few steps behind. He takes my hand and ducks his head to press a quick kiss to my bare shoulder. I shrug away awkwardly, my eyes searching the aisles for Kat. I don't know if she's working here today or at the hospital, but the last thing I want is for her to run into James midshift.

"James," I murmur.

"Sorry." He scratches the back of his neck, his smile fading. "Space, right. It's easier to forget when I'm actually with you."

I nod, turning away from him to grab a box of cereal I don't even like. I read the nutritional facts to avoid his eyes.

"I didn't come here to force you into talking to me," James says. "Not about the future or anything. Your mom just made it sound like a good idea."

"She's not exactly the queen of good ideas."

He frowns at the bitterness in my voice and I realize how rarely we've actually talked these past few weeks. How much my life has changed and how little he actually knows about it now.

I shake my head. Either way, it's too much to talk about in the middle of the cereal aisle. "Me and my mom are just . . . we're just really off right now. And I'm not sure if there's any going back."

Mom and I haven't always gotten along, but we've always

been close. Not talking to her—not feeling understood by her—has been harder than I've let myself realize.

James looks like he wants to hug me, but he doesn't. "I think relationships exist to be screwed up and fixed, if both people are willing to put in the work. I'm sure you'll find your way back to each other."

I bite my lip so my smile isn't as wobbly as it feels. It's such a James thing to say. Sweet and honest and sure. I feel tears stinging my eyes, and he notices before I can blink them away.

"What's wrong?"

"Nothing," I assure him. "You're just . . . a great guy, you know?"

He laughs, looking confused. There's a little crease between his eyebrows. I want to touch it, to see if I can smooth it away. But I draw my hand back just before it nears his face.

TWENTY-SEVEN

"This here's your cousin Maude, and her mama, your other cousin, Jean. And that's little Teddy over there by the food, of course."

Gram introduces us all to a group of people by the tables set up in the park. There's catfish and smoked sausage, grilled chicken and crabs, and macaroni and cheese and greens still hot in their baking pans. There's so much food that I have to actively pay attention to stop myself from drooling.

"Nice to meet you," I say politely, eyes on the crabs.

Gram's in her element. I haven't seen her outside of the house or a hospital room before, but here, by the picnic tables in the middle of Main Street Park, halfway between the group of grills and the basketball court, she's magnetic. Lively, like there's not a sick cell in her body. It's almost impossible to look away. It's more impossible to imagine that someday she'll be gone. A steady flow of people flock toward us, wishing her well and waiting to be introduced to me and reconnect with Mom.

"This is the whole town?" James asks me when I'm able to get away, between forkfuls of collard greens. We got here less than twenty minutes ago, and he already has a plate, made with love and a heavy hand by a middle-aged woman who melted the second he smiled at her.

I had the same thought. There are more people in the park than I've seen in the past month, which is still fewer people than a Saturday morning at the mall back home. "Actually," I say, "I think it's at least two."

He laughs. There's a cool breeze left over from the storm that battles the humidity, so it's just hot instead of muggy. The smell of rain is still in the air, but it's turned out to be a nice day. All around us people are laughing and talking, kids running through the throngs of adults.

Me and James just manage to squeeze to the front when the parade starts. It's not huge, mostly souped-up cars and a half-hearted marching band paired with a dance team, but it's enough to amp up the excitement. The sole drummer tries his best to replicate a drum line before someone hooks up their phone to a huge speaker and the parade quickly turns into a dance party as people two-step their way into the street. An old man with a cane pulls a round-cheeked little girl into a dance; a girl a little younger than me with red, black, and green braids does an interpretive dance with a flag that blurs together in a riot of color. I even catch a quick glimpse of Will as he does a backflip off the hood of a car, laughing as a woman yells at him and drags him out of the crowd.

"You want to dance?" James asks loudly over the music.

I laugh. "Absolutely not." I have a body made specifically for watching other people dance.

"Well, hell, I'll do it for you." Gram appears at my side out of nowhere and takes the hand that James offers.

He hands me his plate and the two of them join the rest of the dancers, James two-stepping the best he can, Gram with her hands on her thighs, dropping into a move so surprising that I nearly double over from laughter. She stays out there even when James has had enough, all of the girls from the original dance team trying to show her a dance that she's quick to pick up. Her laughter eventually blends into the crowd until I can't see her through the rest of the jubilant, moving bodies.

The smell of cinnamon and brown sugar eventually captures my attention, and I pull James away from the dancing and back over to the food, where a group of women are swapping out some of the empty dishes for dessert after dessert. Apple pie, strawberry and rhubarb pie, peach cobbler, and red velvet cake sit next to a watermelon filled to the brim with fruit.

"You pick," I tell James, too indecisive for my own good.

"I'd go with the red velvet. I think Thelma made it this year, and she doesn't mess around when it comes to dessert."

Kat's voice is familiar enough to me that I recognize it even over the sound of celebration. Everything in my body seizes up at the sight of her. It's hard to put her and James in the same thought, let alone the same time and space. The fact that they're both here, looking at me, waiting for me to introduce them, is like something out of an alternate timeline.

It's not that I didn't expect to see her at a party thrown

for the entire town. It's just that I hadn't prepared myself. I'd been so focused on keeping the kiss, and by proxy Kat's entire existence, a secret from James that I didn't even think about what would happen when we ran into her.

It's why I didn't text her. Somehow, I thought that if I didn't put the possibility of them meeting into words, even written words, it wouldn't happen.

But as it turns out, that's not how things work. And even with the shock and panic I feel, my first thought is that I want to be closer to her. I step closer to James instead, like it'll make up for it. Kat catches the movement with quick eyes. Her expression stays exactly the same.

"Kat!" My voice sounds strained. I clear my throat. "This is James. James, this is Kat."

James smiles and sticks out his hand. "Nice to meet you, Kat."

I don't want them to touch. If they touch, somehow, he'll know that I've touched her, too. That I wanted to touch her more.

Kat doesn't shake his hand. She only smiles and takes a sip of her soda. I watch the muscles of her throat work as she swallows. She watches me over the top of the can.

"I've heard a lot about you," she says eventually, eyes flickering back toward James. "Somehow, you always manage to come up."

I laugh. By the grace of every god in existence, it doesn't sound crazed. "You said the red velvet's the best, then?"

"Not the best; I don't want every grandma in Coldwater after me. But it's the one I'd pick."

"I'll take your word for it," James says, chuckling as he reaches for a nearby knife to cut a slice, but I stop him.

"Could you get me a soda, please? Kat's is making me thirsty."

He glances at the cup of sweet tea in my hand but only nods. When he's out of earshot, I move closer to Kat. My heart, in its excitement, leaps. I pitch my voice low. "I didn't know he was coming," I say. It comes out part apology, part excuse.

Kat's polite mask falls away. There's frustration furrowed between her brows, hurt in the downturn of her lips. "But you knew he was here now. You could've texted me. You had literally all day to warn me instead of letting me get blind-sided at the dessert table. This is a hell of a one-eighty from last night."

I grimace guiltily. "I'm sorry. I wouldn't have . . . I mean if I had known . . ." I bite my lip. "Last night shouldn't have happened," I say. I try to sound like I mean it.

"You'd be more convincing if you weren't staring at my lips when you said it."

I jerk away from her, eyes darting back up to meet hers. "Don't say anything to him, Kat. Please."

"Why would I? It's not my secret to tell." She glances over at James, who's gotten caught up in a conversation with some-one's grandfather, nodding along to whatever the silver-haired man is saying. He's holding my soda.

"He's cute," she says. "Tall. Nice smile. That look in his eyes when you say his name. I guess I can see the appeal."

"Kat . . ."

She laughs, but the sound is bitter. "Relax. Seriously, you look like you're gonna have a panic attack." Her smile fades. "You're not, are you?"

I don't know. My head is pounding and my heart is swimming. Or maybe it's the other way around. Every time I take a breath, there's less air. I've been so on edge all day, so focused on keeping James as separate as possible from everything here in town, mainly Kat, that I've barely noticed how high my anxiety's spiked. I want to laugh at my body's response to the consequences of my own actions, but I don't have enough breath for that.

I shut my eyes and feel Kat guiding me onto the bench of a picnic table. Then I feel her hand against my cheek and my eyes spring open. "I'm fine," I say quickly. "James—"

"Isn't paying attention right now. Stop thinking about him," she says, as if that's not what I've been doing this whole summer. "Breathe, okay? Deep breath in to five, hard exhale to ten. Go ahead."

I nod, reluctantly shutting my eyes. I breathe. I feel her sit beside me. "So, I thought about what kind of bird I'd want to be," she says.

"What are you talking about?"

"You asked about birds last night, remember? But you only asked what I'd do. The important question is what kind of bird I'd *be*."

Deep breath.

One. Two. Three.

There are some kids scream-laughing nearby. Kids always do that, blend excitement and fear into a single noise.

Four. Five.

Fun to the point of wildness.

Hard exhale.

"What kind of bird?"

"A Bohemian waxwing. It looks fierce as hell, like it does whatever it wants. Kinda boring-looking at first, all gray and white. But they've got all these little pops of orange and yellow on the wings that surprise you."

I huff out a laugh and it interrupts my rhythm. "Did you look that up?"

"Of course I did," she says, a little defensive. "How many birds do you know off the top of your head?"

"Not many."

"That's what I thought. I looked one up for you, too."

I open my eyes. "Yeah? What kind of bird am I?"

"A sociable weaver."

"A what?"

"A sociable weaver," she repeats. "They're cool actually. They build these huge, permanent nests for their families, like little communities, and generations of birds can live in them for like a hundred years."

I've never heard of that bird, or its nests, but it sounds perfect. Like exactly the kind of bird I'd want to be—one with some sort of permanence. Which means she took what I said to heart, even about something as silly as a bird alter ego. It's so thoughtful I could cry.

"Just how deep into Wikipedia did you get?" I tease instead.

Kat laughs. It's softer than usual, almost embarrassed. "So deep. D'you know birds can get dehydrated? And drunk."

I smile, shaking my head, and Kat smiles in response. "Feel better?"

"Much."

We lock eyes, and for a second, the park fades away. We're back in the lightning bug field and words I can't take back are on my tongue and her face is so, so close to mine . . .

"What did I miss?" James asks. He hands me the soda, then sits across from me and Kat.

"Nothing," I assure him, and Kat agrees, leaning away from me before propping her chin up in her hands. "So, James, Jericka's never mentioned it. How'd you two meet?"

James launches into the story with enthusiasm, peppering in how nervous he was about the new school and playing up Leslie's role as matchmaker. The more James talks, the more Kat smiles along, the guiltier I feel. What the hell is wrong with me that I'm just letting them chat like everything is normal?

I should tell him that we kissed. I *need* to tell him that we kissed. But he looks so happy and he drove all the way here and . . .

". . . right, Jer?"

I blink my way back to the present. "What?"

James and Kat are looking at me expectantly and my heart skips a beat. It's painful, and the next few beats are rapid as it struggles to fall back into rhythm.

"James was just saying how it took him a dozen different

tries to ask you out before you said yes," Kat says. "Why? Were you nervous?"

It's easy to remember just how nervous I was, even if the why eludes me. "Beginnings can be scary," I say after a moment. "Of course I was nervous."

Still, admitting it seems disingenuous somehow. All of the times I've hung out with Kat I've barely hesitated. Maybe the difference is in the intention—dating compared to friendship—but I don't think so. The two of them just bring out very different parts of me.

I take a sip of my soda. The fizz distracts me momentarily, but I nearly choke at the sound of a familiar voice.

"So, you *do* have a boyfriend!"

Will and Mae stride over to us, doubling our little group. Mae scoots into the open space on the other side of Kat while Will perches on top of the table.

"Dude," Will says, grinning. "You're real! I could've sworn the New Girl and Kat were—"

"James," I say quickly, "meet Kat's friends."

While he introduces himself, I steal a glance at Mae. She looks intrigued by James, studying him in that sharp-eyed way of hers. I wonder if Kat told her about last night. I hope she didn't. For once, I want Mae to glare at me so I'll at least know, but she doesn't turn my way.

"It's too bad you only made it down today," Will is saying when I tune back in. "You'd've loved the river party last night; perfect weather and everything. Y'all don't have them where you're from, do you?"

James looks thoughtful for a moment. "Not really, no. People go down the shore for the kind of party you're talking about."

Like the one after his graduation. I'm sure he's remembering what immediately comes to my mind. I take a long sip of my soda, tilting the can back until it obscures my vision.

"So," Mae says, speaking for the first time. "I'm guessing you're going away to school?"

James smiles the bashful smile he always gives when he says, "Yeah. Howard."

She acknowledges the school with a hum. "Down here, then. That'll be hard, won't it? You planning the long-distance thing?"

She turns to stare hard at Kat before smiling sweetly at James. This is her chance to prove that I'm doing exactly what she said I was: having some fling with Kat before I settle down into a long term, possibly long-distance, relationship with James.

And she's right, isn't she?

"We, uh." He glances at me and back to Mae. He's too polite to tell her that it's none of her business, so I step in.

"We haven't talked about it yet actually."

She raises her eyebrows. "Getting late, ain't it?"

I've had enough. Between my hangover and James showing up and him and Kat meeting . . . all of it has made for a hell of a day and it's barely evening.

"You know what, Mae? I think you should stay out of things that don't involve you."

She blinks, clearly surprised. But she's quick to recover. "I think you know exactly how and why I'm involved."

"I don't actually. Because *your* boyfriend? Is sitting right there," I say, pointing to Will. "And anyone else you're worried about at this table is fully capable of making their own decisions without your help."

"Not when they're stupid decisions I'm gonna have to deal with the aftermath of."

We stare hard at each other from across the table. Amid all of the music and chatter around us, our table descends into quiet. James breaks it first. "Jer," he says quietly, "it's fine. She was just curious."

I shake him off. "She's always curious."

I chance a look at Kat. She's leaned in close to Mae, whispering something in her ear. Kat looks up. Our eyes lock for a second before I stand. I need to get away before things go even further south.

"Let's go for a walk," I tell James, grabbing his arm before he can agree. He waves a goodbye to everyone over his shoulder and picks up his pace to match mine as I walk away.

"I was going to congratulate you on making friends," he says when we're far enough away, "but that didn't exactly seem like the case."

I sigh. "Sorry. Me and Mae don't see eye to eye on a good day, and today . . ." I shake my head. "She's basically the worst."

"She's best friends with Kat," he says.

I nod.

"And she doesn't exactly seem keen on the two of you being . . . friends."

There's a slight pause before he says the word, but I'm not

sure if it's real or imagined. Whether it's part of my own guilt or not. I nod again, slower this time.

"You okay?"

James's eyes are steady on mine. He searches my face with a gentleness almost like a caress. He's not oblivious. I know he can tell something is off, but he won't ask. Not outright. And I'm content to use that to my own advantage, I realize. To exist in this space of unasked and unanswered questions.

"I'm fine," I say. Then I shake my head. "Actually, that's a lie. I'm not fine."

I can't let us stay in relationship limbo. James deserves so much more than that. At the very least, he deserves honesty.

"James," I start softly. I will myself to keep my eyes on his. "I—"

"You're going to break up with me," he says. Quiet and sure.

"I'm sorry," I say, tearing up. "How did you know?"

"I figured when you said you needed space. I was just . . . waiting for it."

The furrow in his brows is back and his face holds resignation that tugs at my heart.

"Why didn't you break up with me first?"

"It's not a race. I didn't break up with you because I didn't want to. I figured if you wanted to do it, you would. Or you'd tell me otherwise and we'd make some sort of plan."

I snort a laugh. "That was silly. You've met me—you know how long it takes me to make decisions." I screw my eyes shut. "I'm sorry."

"Hey." He presses the flat of his palm against my cheek. I open my eyes. "Don't feel bad."

It's too late. And I haven't even told him about the kiss yet. His hand against my cheek is warmer than hers was. Rougher. I can't look at him. A beetle the size of my thumb scurries across the dirt. Its black shell looks like a jewel in the sun. I keep my eyes trained on it.

"I kissed Kat."

James stiffens. I feel the tension in his palm, the slight involuntary pressure of his fingers against my cheekbone. He takes a step back. Hurt blooms across his face like a bruise.

"Oh."

"Yeah."

We're quiet, the both of us. This isn't how I meant for all of this to go.

James speaks first, rubbing the back of his neck. "Kat, huh? I didn't realize she was your type."

I nod. Of course, I would go about this whole thing in the most stereotypical bisexual way imaginable—by being a disaster. "I'm so sorry." The only language I seem able to speak right now is apology.

The time that passes in silence feels like days. Like years. When he finally speaks, his voice is miraculously still soft.

"Break up with me."

"I already—" I begin, but James shakes his head.

"No. I guessed. I'm not going to do it for you. If you want this to be over, you have to be the one to end it."

His face drawn with sadness makes him look younger.

Maybe I'm not breaking his heart, but I've cracked it. The thought is enough to make my own ache. But I owe him this much. I take a deep breath.

"You deserve someone who knows what they want, James. Who knows that *you're* what they want. And as much as I care about you and love how patient you are and how easy it is to be with you, I don't . . . I don't think I'm that person. And it's not fair to either of us for me to keep wasting your time and hoping that I might be that person one day." My heart gives a little lurch, but I keep going. "So, I think we should break up."

I press the heels of my hands into my eyes to stop my tears, but it doesn't work. I take deep breaths and wait for them to subside. When they do, James is still there. Silent and watchful.

"We had a good run, huh?"

I've only had a few bad memories with James. Most are scattered arguments over silly things. One involved a traffic stop that had nothing to do with either of us but ended with me crying in a park while he spoon-fed me blackberry ice cream. Another involved a major movie spoiler that made him give me the silent treatment for an entire day. Otherwise, my memory landscape of him is made up of laughter and the easy comfort his presence has always brought me.

"Yeah," I agree, "we had a great run."

I hug him because I can't not. He hugs me back. It's too hot to be so close, but neither of us lets go.

"Listen. I'm upset, sure. And maybe I don't get it. But we're still friends, right?" I nod. "So, I still want you to be happy."

◊

There's something about fireworks. Humans have been to the moon, we fly back and forth across oceans every day, but things bursting with color and noise inspire awe in us like nothing else. If the end of the world was a fireworks display, people probably wouldn't mind it too much.

James and I squeeze through the crowd until we find Mom and Gram. Mom's laughing, sitting surprisingly close to Gram, who's in the middle of a story. I spot Gloria and Asia a few feet away. Asia's phone's up and angled toward the sky. At the edge of the crowd, I catch a glimpse of Kya and Marcus. They're each swinging from one of our dad's arms, giggling as he pulls them up and down like a seesaw. Cora meets my eyes with a soft smile. I haven't talked to either of them since our dinner. I need to do that.

I don't see Kat, but I do my best not to dwell on it.

For a moment, everything is soft. Quiet. Not perfect, not even still, but one of those snapshot moments. The kind cameras can't capture. All of Coldwater is here. All of Coldwater is celebrating.

The first firework—a booming starburst of light—colors the world red.

TWENTY-EIGHT

Coldwater is recovering from the festivities and storms of the week before. I'm still in bed, relying on the grayish light from the windows to help me fiddle with my camera. It's done nothing but get my hopes up, turning on just to turn itself off again a minute later. It's all but ground my photo project to a halt. I've still gone out searching a few times, phone in hand, willing myself to feel as fully as I can. Impatience has taken precedence over everything else on those walks. It's not a feeling that's drawn any echoes my way.

I'm about to unplug the fully charged battery and try again when I hear loud laughter. Mom's *and* Gram's. The twinned sound is enough to get me out of the bed and down the stairs. I step carefully. I'm still unsure of which boards are the creakiest, but I manage to bypass the worst of them just in time to hear Mom ask, ". . . when was this?"

I don't dare risk opening the door, so I press my ear against it instead. The house beyond is muffled but still audible. I hear the friendly honk of a car passing by outside, the constant whirring of the box fan. And I hear Gram and the rustle of something like paper.

"Must've been Miles's fourth, fifth birthday, maybe. Cowboy-themed, but we couldn't get that hat off of him for a good two weeks."

Mom replies, but it's too low for me to make out, only the soft laughter that follows from both of them. I smile at the sound. The first few days after my reconciliation attempt, Mom avoided Gram more than usual, even spending the night at Gloria's. Slowly, though, I've noticed a change. A poured cup of coffee, a slight smile, both of them sitting in the living room together for a prolonged amount of time. Small steps.

I want to see if they're sitting next to each other and if their smiles are as genuine as they sound, but I don't open the door. Even if I am eavesdropping a little, this is their time together.

"Jericka must get the photography thing from you," Mom says. "Before she had a camera, she'd sit and watch anything that caught her eye for minutes at a time. It didn't matter what it was—a rock, a bird, people. Just zone right out until I was yelling her name. Almost got her in trouble a million times until I remembered you looking the same way."

"Me?"

"Yeah. You'd always stop or step back and just . . . stare at stuff. I liked watching you. Trying to figure out what you were seeing. It's no surprise you have all these pictures."

Gram's quiet. When she speaks, her voice is softer. "I take pictures of what I love best in a moment. Makes the remembering easier."

I blink. With all the photos Gram has shown me, I can't believe I never thought to ask her about her favorites. I thought they were all just keepsakes for her—photos of her kids for an album. But maybe she feels like I do: like every picture she takes is a part of her.

I must move too much in my surprise because the stairs give a loud, low groan. The living room goes quiet.

Then I hear Mom's voice. "Jericka?"

I sigh and open the door. "Good morning!" I say, trying to act like I've only just come downstairs.

It doesn't work on either of them. Gram's smile is amused, Mom's is annoyed. They are, in fact, sitting next to each other.

"Good morning yourself," Gram says before Mom can say anything about my eavesdropping. I'm pretty sure she does it on purpose. "Glad you're up; I've got something for you."

"You do?"

Gram stands and makes her way over to me. She's not slow, but there's a tiredness to her movements that wasn't there at the beginning of the summer. It's just the gray day, I assure myself.

"Here," she says, thrusting something into my hands.

Gram is not a sentimental gift giver.

I look down at a camera.

An old Nikon SLR, probably 35 mm film. I've seen them online, read about the shutters and their speed range. I run my hand over the dark frame. The chrome trim has rusted over a little, but it's a beautiful camera, gently used and obviously well cared for. I've rarely shot with film, but somehow it seems fitting, using this old camera in this old, unchanging town.

I look up and open my mouth to thank her, but she waves me away before I can. "Saw you were having trouble with that fancy camera of yours, so I dug this one up. It wasn't doing anybody any favors sitting around here, so you keep it."

"Are you sure?" I ask, though I'm already winding the film forward. There's a moment of resistance that gives me pause, but it's barely a second.

Gram notices. "Film was a little stuck. Had to use an old lead retriever I found, but you should still have a good thirty-four, thirty-five photos."

I don't know what that is, and I'm too eager to try out the camera to ask.

"Let's make it one less, then. Can I?"

When she nods, I lift the camera to my face.

In a way, it's a mirror of the earlier photos I took. Them sitting close together and looking at me. But this time, I didn't ask them to. This time, it's not posed. This feels like the first real picture I've taken of Mom with her mom. For a moment, I'm all too aware of the generations that led us here. All that kinship and love that brought us all into being. And everything else, too.

I snap the picture. As the shutter releases, I come to the realization that one day, I will lose them both. But Gram is right—the picture will make the remembering easier.

I avoid Kat after James leaves and the storms blow over. For a day. Two. Three. A week passes, and I spend most of it with Gram and Mom, watching old movies and fiddling with my new camera and trying, simply, not to sweat to death. Gram had a chemo off-week, so there were no hospital visits. I even talked my way out of trips to Food Lion.

Chemo starts back up on a Wednesday. It's a day Kat usually has off, so I don't think too much about running into her. But when I walk into the café, there she is: braids pulled up into a heavy bun, dark apron knotted loosely around her waist. We blink at each other. She speaks first.

"Hey."

"Hi."

An awkward silence falls, and neither of us rushes to fill it. I should apologize for what happened with Mae. I should tell her about James. But I don't say anything. And the longer I'm quiet, the more she searches my face with her careful, constant stare as if everything I'm not saying is written on my face instead.

C'mon, Jericka. Don't be a coward.

Kat turns away from me, toward the espresso machine. If I don't say something right now, I'm going to screw everything up worse than I already have.

"I'm sorry about yelling at Mae."

Inwardly, I groan. It's not what I want to say, but the words sit so much easier on my tongue.

She glances at me and shrugs. "She yells at a lot of people herself. I don't think she took it too personally."

"Right. But the thing is . . . she was right." I bite my lip. "I've been treating you like you're a distraction or a fling, especially when James showed up, and that isn't fair to you. It's not fair, and it isn't even true. Kat, you . . ."

Her eyes are on me now. And it feels like this is it.

No more indecisiveness.

"I don't know what we're doing. Or what happens next. Or even what I *want* to happen next. And usually, I'd be terrified, but . . . it doesn't bother me."

At her raised eyebrows, I laugh.

"Okay, it doesn't bother me *that* much. Because time doesn't feel like a real thing with you. It's just you and me and the present. And even when my brain sucks and everything starts creeping back in, you smile at me or say something so stupid that I can't help but laugh, and it all settles back down."

I'm pretty sure I'm rambling or making a fool of myself or both. But I'm also finally being honest.

"That's . . ." Kat huffs. She stares at me like she's waiting for a punch line. "What the hell am I supposed to say to that?"

I shrug, feeling a little off-kilter. "You don't have to say anything. I just . . . thought you should know. Well, that, and I broke up with James."

"You broke up with him," she repeats.

I nod, and she taps her fingers along the counter, fingernails flashing a chipped purple. Is she nervous or am I projecting? Now I've puked up my feelings all over, and I really wouldn't blame her if she's uncomfortable. At the river party, there was plausible deniability for both of us. That's not an option for me now, but I'll let her take it if she wants.

We can pretend like all of this never happened. I definitely won't ever think about the feeling of her lips on mine or how the glow of the lightning bugs was so much like candlelight or—

"I didn't ask you to," she says finally.

My heart falls.

"But I won't lie; I'm glad you did."

My heart picks up again so quickly I'm surprised I don't faint. We smile at each other like fools until Kat asks, "What now?"

"We have the rest of the summer," I say. "We can play things by ear. I mean, if you want to."

Kat studies my face before stretching her hand out toward me, pinkie extended. "Okay," she says. "Deal."

I loop my pinkie around hers without a second thought. It's nice, not hesitating for once. "Deal."

I tug her forward and she meets me over the counter in a kiss. There's no fire like the other night, no deep burning in my veins that urges me toward her. I'm a little clumsy, even. But there is softness—the feel of her mouth on mine—and sweetness like artificial cherries.

TWENTY-NINE

"I got in."

Kat's voice is a whisper on the other end of my phone too early the next morning. In the dark of my attic room, she might as well be an echo looming by my bed. I click on the light and rub the sleep from my eyes.

"What?"

"I got in," she says again, louder. And again, until the words get lost in her laughter and excitement. Until they finally register in my brain.

She got into Hampton.

I sit up. "Holy shit."

"I know!" She makes a noise that sounds so close to squealing it makes me grin. I let her excitement wake me up and foster some of my own.

"Congratulations! How'd you find out at"—I pull the phone away from my face to check the time—"three thirty-six in the morning?"

"I checked my email. Well, I mean, earlier I checked their website. And their Instagram. And their Twitter. And they said they might start sending out final acceptances for wait-list kids soon, so I kept refreshing the page."

She's giddy with excitement. The only point of reference I have for her house is her living room, filled with people, so I try to picture her in her room instead, lying in bed, her phone pressed to her cheek as she grins up at the ceiling.

"Sorry I woke you up. I should've just texted, but . . . I needed to tell someone in the moment, y'know?"

I get it. This is her dream. It's hard keeping dreams to yourself when they come true, and I'm glad to be the person she chose to share this with. "Don't be sorry," I say. "I'm happy for you."

"Thanks." Her voice is hushed now, like the acceptance is finally sinking in. "Do you want to go for a drive?"

I fight a yawn. "A drive?"

"It's the only way I'll get to sleep at this point."

"Sure." There's no way I'm leaving her to drive around alone in the dark.

She brightens. "I'll be there in ten."

It's nothing to slip out of the house ten minutes later, though I pause in the kitchen to leave a note in case Mom or Gram realizes I'm gone. It won't be enough to get me out of trouble if they do, but it'll save Mom a heart attack.

Kat grins at me when I settle into the passenger seat. Her braids are tied back in a lopsided ponytail and there are deep circles beneath her eyes I've never seen before, but she's almost vibrating with energy.

"Well? You gonna show me the acceptance letter or what?"

The smile she gives me makes my heart stutter. She tosses her phone my way and I quickly scan the email.

Dear Kathleen . . . Congratulations on your acceptance . . . awarded an undergraduate merit scholarship . . .

I jerk my head up and come face-to-face with her grin. "Kat! You got a *scholarship*?"

She laughs. "I'm shocked, too. I was fully prepared to dive headfirst into debt."

Her accent is thicker than normal, and with the tired rasp of her voice, it's incredibly endearing. I lean over to hug her. She's warm and smells like soap.

"So, where are we going?"

Rocks crunch beneath the tires as she reverses out of my driveway and shoots down the road. "Wherever we want."

We roll down our windows and breathe in deep, pulling in fresh air that tastes of nighttime. We're on a stretch of particularly winding roads, up and then down a hill. Down a long, straight road flanked on either side by cornfields.

"I'm actually getting out of Coldwater," Kat whispers. Wind whips her voice out the window, so she sticks her head out, too. "I'm getting out of here!" she yells into the night, and I smile, even as I eye the road ahead warily. I try not to ruin the moment, but I only let myself breathe again when all of her is safely back in the car.

She glances my way and laughs at whatever expression she sees on my face. "You should try it."

"I don't think I have any good news I need to tell the world."

"Maybe it has something to tell you."

I snort and she grins beside me. In the middle of the night, with no makeup and in baggy sweats, she's unfairly beautiful. "Cheesy as it sounds—"

"And it sounds incredibly cheesy."

"Cheesy as it sounds," she repeats, "I mean it. Night drives always clear my head. The wind, the fresh air, the sky, the speed. It's the perfect combination."

I bite my lip. "You won't take your eyes off the road?"

"Not for a second."

"Or your hands?"

In response, Kat's loose grip on the wheel tightens.

I stick my head out before panic can take over and shut my eyes. Almost immediately, I feel like one of those flowers that bloom at night, fueled by the moon. I can feel its light on my face. The wind is in my hair, whistling in my ears as Kat presses on the gas. I breathe in and lean out farther, until the edge of the window presses into my stomach, holding me in place.

I don't know where we're going, and for the moment, I don't care. There's only the wind and the moon and the car. And Kat, laughing as she urges us forward into the unknown even faster.

When she stops at a rare red light, Kat's aglow in it. She

looks joyful and wild and tired, and my hands itch so badly for a camera that it's almost painful. But with how sharp everything feels, I know I don't need a picture to remember tonight. I lean over the console and kiss her quick, just as the light turns green. And then we're moving forward again, aimless on a warm summer night.

"I think," she says over the rush of wind, "we should go to the old schoolhouse."

THIRTY

"Right now?"

The Kat sitting next to me can't possibly be the same one who refused to even let me take her picture because my project involved echoes. Her Hampton acceptance has changed her brain because *that* Kat would never suggest going to a schoolhouse full of ghosts at any time, let alone in the middle of the night.

But this Kat just nods.

"This project's important to you, right? It's your ticket somewhere else, and if I can help you with that, if you need the help, then I will." She nods again as if she's reaffirming her decision. "I want to."

"Are you sure? What about what happened last time?" As much as I would love not being alone when I finally step foot in there, I'm not a fool. Kat is on an emotional high, probably willing to say or do anything that might make me feel as good as she does right now.

"I'm sure," she says.

It's a sweet gesture, that in the middle of her own happiness she would think so fully about mine. But I'm not going to take advantage of it.

"Considering what happens to all the Black people in every scary movie I've seen, how about we take a rain check? And if you still want to go with me tomorrow, we can go. I don't want to ruin your night by making it about me."

Kat smiles. "You couldn't ruin it," she says as she makes a quick U-turn. "But fine."

I have a vague idea of where we are, but the dark turns everything into shadows. Still, I'm surprised when we end up back at my house a few minutes later, Kat killing the lights before she comes to a stop.

"I'm not going to change my mind," she murmurs. I lean in to kiss her goodbye. I mean for it to be quick, but we both linger. Her lips move gently over mine as she speaks. "Tomorrow. First thing. I'll meet you there."

I nod, knowing I won't hold her to it if she doesn't show up. "Congratulations again, Kat. You deserve it."

◊

She shows up the next morning with a flashlight, a cross around her neck, and two still-steaming cups: hot chocolate for me, coffee for her.

I want to ask if she's sure about this, and reassure her that she can back out, no strings attached.

Instead, I say, "How are you so awake right now?"

She grins, bouncing on the balls of her feet. "This is my second coffee today."

Right. I take a sip of hot chocolate, the flush of warmth pleasant despite the heat, but the sugar is slow acting, and I don't feel any more awake than I did on my walk out here.

"Okay," Kat says, stuffing her free hand into her pocket. "Let's get in there before I lose my nerve."

She strides toward the burnt-out building with purpose, but I touch her elbow before she can get more than a few feet. "You don't have to come in with me. Especially not just for my project."

At this point, I'm not even sure *I* want to go in. The thought of my own feelings being projected back at me on a loop is enough to make my hands shake. Feelings exist to be felt—but also moved past. I've witnessed it, on its own loop, in Mom, in Gram, in their slow path toward reconciliation. They'd focused so deeply on their feelings for each other, and holding on to them, for so long that it was hard for them to see beyond them.

Who was Mom without her anger? Who was Gram without her guilt? I'm not sure they know yet. But I think they're far closer to figuring it out now than they were before.

Can the same be said for the echoes? That's what I want to know, what feels even more important than just taking pictures of them.

Are they alive because of their grief? Or is grief all that they are?

It's such a huge ask. Such a large thought. And it's not really all that tied to photos anymore, if I'm being honest, except that photography is part of my thought process. I'm hoping a new thought will spark with every click of my shutter and, if I'm lucky, I can turn whatever photos result into some sort of visual narrative.

I'm not sure how I'm going to go about getting answers. But even if I were, I can't get them out here. If this is home for the echoes, then inside is where they'll be.

Kat's been quiet. I'm not sure if she was waiting for me to unravel my thoughts or wrestling with her own but, with her back to me, she takes a deep breath. I watch the slow rise and heavy fall of her shoulders. "I know I don't have to."

It's all she says before she starts walking again.

The weight of Gram's camera in my hands, the strap around my neck, are comforting. I follow her.

It doesn't smell like smoke or fire inside, just dirt and rotting wood. I wonder how it used to smell, when it was a school and not a burial ground.

I want to know this place. Who built it. Who walked the halls and trailed their hands along the walls. Which kids sat in the front and which ones talked throughout their entire lesson. Those things are impossible for me to know or experience in the way that I want, but the women who remember it are here.

Somewhere, anyway.

I expected it to be crowded with echoes from the moment we stepped inside, but all I see are the half-burnt carcasses of desks and dozens of dead flies. Everything is silent here. The kind of silence that doesn't belong to the daytime. I shiver, though the sun is warm on my arms and the crown of my head, where it pours in from the roof and great gaps in the walls.

Kat must feel the strangeness, too. "D'you know they have these little legs for dorm beds that make them taller?" she asks. "Mae thinks I should loft my bed when I get to Hampton, but there's no way I wanna be that close to the ceiling or high enough up to fall outta bed every morning."

She barely pauses to give me space to respond. I've never heard her ramble before. I'd be intrigued if my nerves weren't on such high alert. I use my camera like a telescope, seeing the world through its tiny square as we inch forward. There are a surprising amount of shadows and dark corners for it to still be morning.

But everything is normal.

No echoes. Not even any mice.

It's almost boring.

I take pictures anyway. The dusty keys of a one-legged piano. A soot-blackened stove in the middle of the room, pipe extended upward into a roof that's barely there. A shot from the front, where a teacher might stand to look at her class, now a mess of dirt and warped metal.

It's all so . . . sad.

I feel it settle into the soil of me and plant roots. Tiny shoots of sadness already up and coming.

Despite the sunlight pouring in from every hole or missing bit of roof, it's still dark. Too dark for any of the answers I've convinced myself are here, in piles of dirt and twisted and broken metal. Too dark for pictures of any real substance.

No photography programs for you, Jericka. No videography classes or fun editing software. Nope, you get to keep apartment-hopping around New Jersey with your mom like a wanted criminal, taking pictures of every new room you have like a ten-year-old with an iPhone while everyone else goes to their dream schools and forgets you even exist.

I tighten my grip on my camera, trying to find solid mental ground.

"Hampton's got this thing," Kat says, close enough to me that I jump. I didn't realize I'd tuned out so thoroughly or that she was still talking. "This huge party for Black History Month that's supposed to blow Howard Homecoming out of the water . . ."

"That's great," I murmur, fiddling with my camera. Maybe when she's in Virginia she'll forget we were ever here together. She'll cut me out of the stories she tells her new friends and amp up the creepiness for fun. "Hampton is super great. You're in. You're going. You're excited and you love it. *I get it.*"

"Yeah," she says slowly, irritation seeping into her voice. "I do love it and I *am* excited. I thought you were happy for me."

I grit my teeth. "I am! But I don't want to hear about it right this second. It's just . . ."

It's just coming up so soon. If we're playing this whole thing by ear, what does that mean? Am I going to be left behind? So tied to Coldwater in her head that she shoves me into a box labeled PAST as she eagerly unpacks the boxes of her future in her new dorm room?

I feel the tears sting my eyes before they blur my vision.

Maybe Mae was right, but she had things backward. What if this is a fling for Kat? Some final hurrah before she goes to college and meets college girls from places a hundred times more interesting than the suburbs of *New Jersey* . . .

I wince against a sharp pain in my temple. "You don't have to keep talking about it. You don't have to keep acting like leaving home is the best thing that's ever happened to you."

"It *is*."

I look up finally. She's backlit by the sun. I want to take a picture, but I know it will be overexposed. I'm not sure I want to remember this exact moment, anyway, where all Kat wants is to leave and all I want to do right now is scream.

"Maybe that's a problem, Kat! All you ever do is blame Coldwater, but maybe it's you who's the problem."

"You think I'm selfish for having dreams that live outside of this town?"

"No. But I do think you're running away." I think of Mom. How when her fear of being stuck was set against her love for me, that fear won. "What's so wrong with being stuck here? In Coldwater, where the town itself and the people tied to it even in death love you. Not to mention your friends and your family and—" I catch myself. "Why do you need more than that?"

The words are on my tongue and in my voice, but they don't feel like mine. They're tied to a desperation I'm not sure I've ever felt.

"Who *wouldn't* need more than that? You love it here so much?" Kat laughs. "Fine. You stay. But don't tell me that I shouldn't have bigger dreams than this stupid, haunted town just because my family is here."

My head is throbbing now, in the sockets of both eyes and at both temples. "You're just going to leave them behind, then."

"People leave places, Jericka! It doesn't mean they're abandoning everyone they love. People move. They travel. They drift." Her frown softens and the rest of her face softens with it. For a moment, she just looks lost. "It's not right to be trapped in one place. Do you understand? It's not fun or cute or homey. It just sucks."

I shut my eyes against the migraine trying to burrow into my brain. I want to argue with her, but I don't know why. *I'm happy she's leaving*, I try to remind myself. The thought fades as easily as it forms.

She can't leave.

Of course she can't.

What about me?

What about *us*?

My eyes spring open.

There are so many of them, so suddenly. One, five, a dozen.

"Kat," I whisper. "Echoes."

I don't know where they were lingering before, but they crowd around us now like a mob, pressing closer and closer until I can barely breathe for the cold that clings to me.

I'm not sure Kat was standing next to me before, but her hand is in mine now, squeezing tight enough to ache. I can't see her face, but I can feel her pulse in her palm, quick as mine. At first, all I can do is stare at the echoes. Searching desperately for the possible spark of humanity that drove me here in the first place.

The good news is: There's plenty of it.

That's the bad news, too.

Every face I see is scrunched up in pain or wide-eyed with panic or blank with resignation. Some women are crying, or at least look like they are. There's no sound besides me and Kat's ragged breathing, and that makes it all so much worse. Silent screams and silent tears, pleading eyes and muffled panic.

There's so much emotion.

Too much of it.

Loneliness

and

irritation

and

longing

and

desperation

and

anger

and

fear

and

hopelessness

and, and, and.

I raise my camera to my face with my free hand. It's not a shield, but it helps anyway, narrowing my world so I can only take in one anguished face at a time. My finger's on the shutter button, but I'm not even sure if I'm snapping. I'm just watching. Taking them in one by one. Their emotions don't feel so overwhelming with the heavy weight of a camera and its lens between us. They don't feel quite so new, so present.

Because they're not, I realize.

The echoes might have latched onto me and Kat and all our present-day feelings, but there is nothing immediate in their grief. Their tragedy happened over a century ago. Their pain is nothing but memory.

They're nothing but memory.

Memories they embody and play on a loop, drawing in anyone looking for some sort of connection, anyone who lets themselves get too close, like a fisherman's lure. I'm not sure it's intentional, but intention rarely matters.

Stay, a chorus of voices urge, voices like thunder. *Stay.*

They're passing on their grief to women in town like a disease, like an inheritance.

"I don't want it," I whisper.

I can't hear my own voice, but I focus on the shape of it in my mouth to remind myself that I have one. *I'm* not just a memory, even as the echoes' pain digs deep, as their awful memories try to bring all of mine to the surface.

It's a breathless, burning feeling that nearly brings me to my knees, but I grip the camera tighter. Grip Kat's hand tighter, too, using my viewfinder as I retrace our steps back toward where we came from, back outside, leading us back to the present.

THIRTY-ONE

The echoes have a long reach.

After all, there's nothing keeping them in the schoolhouse. Coldwater is theirs to explore at will, and they do so. I feel them at my back, hear their pleas bouncing around in my skull and echoing in my ears. They don't allow room for any other thought.

Not unless I click the shutter.

With every flash of the camera, so unnecessary in the daylight, I get a second's clarity. If I can just get us to the car, we should be okay inside.

I hope.

I don't dare turn around, but I glance out of the corner of my eye at Kat. She's glassy-eyed and silent, but she's conscious enough to still hold tight to my hand, and that's what is important. The car is so close. A few dozen feet away at the most.

"We're almost there," I assure us both.

It's hard. So, so hard. I try to focus on happy memories to offset the grief: getting my first camera, dragging James and Leslie to junior prom, losing to Kya and Marcus at Mario Kart, catching Gram and Mom talking to each other with smiles on their faces, watching Kat laugh in the sunshine.

Happiness ripples through the emotional tide of my thoughts, slow at first, then big enough to drown everything else. For a moment, even the echoes pause.

It gives me just enough time to lower my camera, dig the keys out of Kat's pocket, and unlock the doors. I open the passenger-side door and lightly shove her in before running around to the driver's side. I slam my door shut, then reach over to pull hers closed, too. I lock them.

We wait in silence. The pressure in my head, the slithering voices, fade slowly. Only an eerie sadness lingers.

I know the feeling isn't fully my own, but logic has never helped me deal with my emotions before.

"Well, that sucked," Kat says. Her voice is so soft. So is my laugh.

"Definitely worse than I thought it might be," I agree.

She glances down at the camera around my neck. "Did you manage to take any pictures, at least?"

I snapped more than I probably should have, but I doubt there's anything salvageable on the film. "Sort of," I say.

I glance at the frame counter on the top right. Surprisingly, there's one shot left.

"I'll be right back."

Kat stares at me. "What? Are you—"

I unlock the door and slip out. I'm more than aware what a bad idea this is even as I do it anyway, stepping away from the safety of the car and closer to the emotional chaos of the schoolhouse.

I can feel the ripples of a few remaining echoes, catch their outlines in shimmering rays of sunlight. The sadness sparks back to life, but it's far more muted than before. I don't know if they're holding back or if I've adapted to it, but I'm grateful for the reprieve.

I lift the camera to my face again.

Already the leniency is fading, pain and grief threatening to creep back in. I grit my teeth and focus my lens on an echo farther away, turned halfway from me. From what I can make out, she's an older woman, wrinkles in the downturn grooves of her mouth, her stare endless.

I set the aperture and play with the shutter speed. All these weeks and I still haven't nailed the settings I'm supposed to use when trying to capture an echo. Should I go with a low f-stop like a portrait, or will she get lost in the background blur? Is the sun going to wash everything out anyway? I try not to think about it too hard as I snap, using up my last bit of film.

"Okay," Kat says from behind me. I turn to see her window barely cracked, her face all but pressed against the glass. "Let's get out of here, please. I feel a migraine bigger than this whole damn town forming."

I'm starting to, too. I nod and make my way back around, slipping into the driver's seat. She's still turned in the direction of the schoolhouse, even when I start the car.

"Kat? You want me to drive?"

She's slow to tear her gaze away. "Please."

I start to switch gears, but I pause when her hand covers mine.

"That was a lot," she says.

"It was."

"Are you okay?"

"I think so." I pause, lifting my eyes from her hand to her face. "Are you? That couldn't have been easy after what happened when you were younger . . ."

I trail off. I should have thought about that before we went in. I should've told her to not come, or at least to stay in the car. Not that she would've listened.

The smile she gives me is faint—exhausted—but it's there.

"No," she says. "But I will be. I feel like I understand it a little more, at least."

"The echoes?"

"The grief."

Her hand slides off mine as she leans back in her seat, shutting her eyes. I pull forward, going slower than even this long, empty road demands, and drive until the schoolhouse is no longer visible in the rearview.

Even this far away, I'm not fully settled. There's lingering noise, residual grief.

My own memories.

THIRTY-TWO

All I want is something greasy from the diner, a hot bath, and a gallon of ice cream. But I settle for the spot on the couch next to Gram when Kat drops me off. We'd ended up driving forty-five minutes to Delaware, both to get out of town for a moment and to drop the film off at a shop specializing in film processing. I'm honestly not sure how the pictures will turn out, but I want to know as soon as possible.

Maybe they'll be pitch-black and overexposed.

Maybe there will be echoes.

There's nothing I can do about it now, though, so I just rest my head on Gram's shoulder. She turns to me with raised eyebrows.

We sit there for a few breaths until she asks, "What's gotten into you?"

"About a dozen different emotions," I mutter, burying my face into her shoulder. I've never been this close to her. She's warm and solid, but so thin now that I worry if I lean too heavily against her, I could break something. Even here, she smells like the hospital.

"Spirits?" she asks.

I nod. "Me and Kat went to the schoolhouse."

"Don't sound like a smart plan to me so far."

"It wasn't too bad, actually. Not at the end."

"What about the rest?"

I frown at the thought. The echoes might have influenced and amplified things, but they couldn't put words in our mouths. Everything we said to each other—that was us. I explain as much to Gram.

She eyes me quietly, then grabs the blanket on the other side of her and hands it to me. I wrap it around my shoulders. It's too hot for a blanket, but it feels a bit like being hugged.

"The one thing spirits are good at," she says finally, "is making sure you know how you're really feeling. And no one likes coming face-to-face with that. It gets real unpleasant real fast. You should've expected that."

"What, an argument?"

"Reality. Your feelings don't change hers about wanting to leave and vice versa. Whether that's a problem or not . . . well. You got it all out, didn't you? And you're both still standing."

I nod. "Ran out of film, though."

"Already? Thirty-five shots in that old place—how many you think are actually gonna develop?"

"I don't know. I guess we'll see."

She nods. "Lucky for you I've got more of the film lying

around here. Not sure if any of it's still good, but it's there. Go check in my left-hand drawer by the bed."

I squirm reluctantly out of the warmth of the blanket, my mind still on the argument as I go. It's not like me and Kat ended on a bad note. But I know just how easily the things we shove down can get dredged up again, and I'm nervous. Not so much for what happens next, but for how this all might end. Everything has an end, after all. But maybe summer is summer and it's allowed to be its own thing without affecting the rest of the year.

I try to keep that in mind as I take the new film, two canisters, up to my room, then head down to cozy up beside Gram again.

She nudges me out of my thoughts the second I sit down.

"I had a movie all queued up before you got here. You wanna watch or you wanna wallow?"

I glance at the TV. It's paused on the title screen of a movie I've never seen. "Who's in it?"

"Eartha. Sammy Davis Jr. Couple others."

I purse my lips in thought, then settle back into the love seat, pulling the blanket tighter around me. "I'll watch."

She laughs and reaches for the remote. I try not to notice her sharp breath and her trembling hand as she presses play.

Twenty minutes later, she's asleep and my mind is back on the schoolhouse. Memories are meant to be remembered, and that's what I want for the echoes, despite everything. But how can I manage that if they don't show up on film?

I sigh, rewinding the tape and shutting it off so we can

finish tomorrow. I consider waking Gram and helping her to bed, but she looks content where she is, buried in blankets, so I head upstairs to my room.

In bed, I'm still trying to think of the best way to immortalize a group of dead women who do more harm than good when my phone vibrates. I answer on instinct. It's only ever Leslie or Mom, and Mom rarely calls when she's out with Gloria. To my surprise, Kat's voice pours from the tiny speaker.

"You think if I gave myself an exorcism I would die?"

The question startles a laugh out of me. "Did an echo possess you when I wasn't looking?"

"Nah, but it's like a cleanse, right?"

"I'm not sure that's how that works. I also don't think you can exorcise yourself."

"So, you're telling me I should stand up in the middle of Sunday service and ask Pastor Malcolm instead? I will, but if my dad asks, I'm blaming you."

I laugh again.

"I feel like my body's still vibrating from the whole thing."

I sigh. "I know what you mean. I'm sorry I made you go."

"I'm pretty sure it was my idea."

"But I brought it up first."

"Jericka, I can make my own decisions. If I want to go into a schoolhouse that's the stuff of my literal nightmares because this cute girl wants to go, I'm pretty sure that's my choice."

"Kat . . ."

"Do you think everything that someone does is somehow your fault?"

I grimace. That's not as far from the truth as I'd like it to be. "No, but—"

"Good. I could've stayed home and slept in, but I didn't. So, like I said, my choice."

"But we argued."

"We talked. Maybe a little louder than we needed to. But I said what I had to say and you said what you had to. Unless you have more to say?"

"No."

"Great! Then we're good."

I groan, rolling onto my back. The ceiling's peeling and water-stained in a handful of places. "How are you so nonchalant about everything?"

She snorts. "I think we were emotional enough today."

We're both quiet, but it's our normal quiet. The slightly charged, familiar one that always makes me feel like one of us is on the verge of suggesting something stupid and exciting.

I sigh. I still don't know what comes next, now or at the end of the summer.

It's the worst feeling. It's the best feeling.

"So?" she says finally. "Exorcism: yay or nay?"

◊

I go for a walk. It seems like a better idea than taking a nap or wasting a new film canister with test shots because I'm still worried I'm overexposing or underexposing every photo.

It's ridiculously hot out and my shirt clings to my skin, but every breeze brings relief and the smell of a distant barbecue. It only takes half an hour and a couple miles before I find myself outside my dad's house. The swing on the front porch brings up memories that I swallow, but it's Marcus and Kya, playing tag in the front yard, who catch my attention.

Kya runs toward me with a grin. I brace myself for a hug. Instead, she slaps my hand and keeps running, giggles trailing behind her.

"You're it!"

"The mailbox is base!" Marcus says, quick behind Kya, though still close enough to tag if I wanted to. He turns to me, sticking out his tongue as he jogs backward. "Unless you're too slow?"

That's it. No *hellos*, no *why are you heres*, no questions about me storming out last time.

I smile. Then I sprint after them.

THIRTY-THREE

We play tag until I'm sweating and it's hard to catch my breath. I'm leaning against the steps to try and do so when Cora comes out with a few water bottles. She gives one to Kya and one to Marcus, then sinks onto the step beside me, holding out the last one.

She smiles. "Long time, no see."

My own smile is wary. "I know. I'm sorry. About how I left the last time and—"

"Don't apologize, Jelly Bean. It was a lot. It'd be a lot for anyone."

I nod.

"I don't blame you if you're still angry with us," she continues. "You have every right to be, both for our secrets and for the fool way your dad decided to spill them. But I hope you know that you're family and that you're always welcome here."

I try to let her words settle into the space inside me that needs to hear them. They don't quite plant roots, but they fit.

"Where did that nickname come from?" I ask. It's been on my mind, the nickname and the easy way it rolls off her tongue. Even Mom only calls me Jer.

Her smile softens. "You were so tiny when we met, and so wriggly. Like a little jumping bean but sweeter. Jelly Bean was just the first thing I thought of."

"You weren't upset when I showed up?" When I was dropped off so suddenly, rather. "It wasn't . . . weird for you? Having to be a mom to someone else's kid when you were so young?"

She thinks a minute, eyes drifting toward the front yard where Kya and Marcus are back to running around, water bottles empty and abandoned. "Maybe for about half a second. I'd been with Gerard since you were born, damn near, so I'd spent plenty of time with you. Me and Lacey had even been friendly, back in school. But I looked at it like this: You had a mama and I wasn't her. But as long as you were with me, I'd treat you like my own baby."

I take a long sip of water. "I'm sorry I don't remember."

Cora bumps her shoulder against mine. "No apologies, remember? Besides. We've got the rest of our lives to get reacquainted, if you're willing. Whenever you're ready." She stands, bending to press a kiss to the top of my head. She raises her voice as she straightens up. "You two come inside and wash up for lunch, now! I don't wanna see no filthy hands at my table."

She looks back at me and her smile turns teasing. "That goes for you, too, if you're coming."

◊

"Jericka?"

I glance up from the coloring book Kya and I are sharing to see Dad lowering himself to sit beside us. She spares a bright smile for him but immediately goes back to coloring in a mermaid's tail. I set aside my grinning, creepy bear. I don't know what to say. It's like our first meeting all over again, but worse. We have history now: the painful one that I remember and the happy one that I don't.

"Hi."

"Hi."

He inhales deeply and takes off his hat to wipe sweat from his head. Without it, he looks surprisingly young. I can see Marcus in him. "I'm sorry," he says. "About what I said *and* how I acted. I shouldn't have sprung everything on you that night and let you walk off alone. Everything had been weighing on me so long that I . . ." He shakes his head. "I shouldn't have put all that on you just to get it off my chest. It wasn't fair of me to burden you like that."

"It wasn't," I agree. "I was there for dinner, to get to know all of you. If you really felt that guilty this whole time, you could've told me before. Over the phone. In a letter. You could've even come to visit. You had fourteen years and a million chances."

He nods, not looking at me. "I know."

"But I appreciate the calls. And the texts." I've ignored them, but I did appreciate them. "I don't forgive you. You *or* Mom." I still have too many questions for that. And, yeah, I'm still pretty pissed. But I also don't want to be like Gram. I don't want to be like Mom. Never talking, never connecting, just staying stuck in my own disconnection and disappointment. "Not yet, at least."

The smile he gives me is a little sad and a little hopeful.

I remember a question I've been meaning to ask since Gram brought out her pictures. "Do you, um, do you have any photos? I mean, from when I lived here?"

"Of course we do," Dad says, giving my shoulder a squeeze.

Kya, Marcus, and Cora join us when Dad pulls out a stack of photo albums. The year is scribbled on the front-left inside corner of each one with a Sharpie.

It's strange, seeing the evolution of myself from a baby to a toddler and even stranger to look at that younger self in places and with people I don't remember. My siblings are quick to point out the people I don't recognize, though, and they rush to a bookshelf for newer albums, showing me older versions of the same people. Shared experiences years apart. Dad and Cora are good storytellers, too, weaving backstories for every snapshot, like my mini meltdown at my third birthday party or Marcus's stage fright at a school concert.

There's a Mom-shaped emptiness in me while I look at the pictures, of course. But I think of our albums at home. Of all the pictures she's in, that we're in together—just the two of us.

I'm full by the time it's time for me to leave—with sand-wiches and sweet tea and childhood stories.

"Don't be a stranger," Cora murmurs as she hugs me goodbye.

"We'll see you soon," Dad promises. His hug is long and he rests a hand on the back of my head, like cradling a baby.

"Are you coming back?" Kya asks, looking up at me. She's clinging to my leg while Marcus stands nearby, awkward and unsure in that little-boy way of his.

"I will."

"Tomorrow?"

I laugh. "Maybe not that soon."

"The next day?"

She keeps it up, shouting days of the week at me in her tiny, high-pitched voice until I'm out the front door, then on the porch, then too far away to hear her.

THIRTY-FOUR

I need portraits of people for my portfolio, not just the over-exposed interior of a burnt schoolhouse and weirdly shaped sunspots I'm assuming will be on the film that I get back, so I ask Gram to pick a spot where I can take her photo. I expect her to choose one of her usual haunts, the living room or the porch. Instead, she tells me to grab Mom's keys.

The drive is surprisingly long, but every time I ask where we're going, she only tells me to keep straight or make this left or watch for the cars ahead of me.

Traffic is heavier outside of Coldwater. Angry horns blasting, impatient people speeding, and, eventually, I figure out why. We're en route to Ocean City—and so is everyone else.

Gram has me pull over when the Ferris wheel is visible in the distance, the huge circle at odds against the flat skyline.

"You ever get on that?" I ask once we're out of the car.

"Not a fan of heights. Or boardwalks."

I glance at her. "Probably not the best place to come, then."

"Good thing we're not here for either one."

This far from the boardwalk it's just old beach houses and sand. The sea breeze brings salt and cold air, and I shut my eyes for a second to savor it. I haven't been to the beach all summer. We're only forty-five minutes away, double that with traffic, but it's so different from Coldwater. Seagulls squawk overhead and sand finds its way between my toes. There are no ghosts in sight and not a single person who recognizes me or knows my parents.

"Go grab me one of them chairs," Gram says suddenly. She's wig-less today, like she has been more and more lately, and her natural hair is short. It curls around her ears, dark brown and gray that flashes silver in the sunlight.

I pull two abandoned beach chairs over to her and she sinks into the nearest one with a heavy sigh. I expect her to lie back, but she doesn't. She just sits on the edge and watches the waves roll in and out.

"We met on the beach," she says finally. "This beach. And it was close enough that we brought the kids here later. Made sandcastles, played in the water, even ate sandwiches under our towels to keep the birds from bothering us." She turns to me with teary eyes and a soft smile. "We were happy here. Even if things were falling apart on the way here or on the way back. *Here* was different. Safe."

She turns back toward the water, and I ready my camera as quietly as I can. Portraits are good, but I've always been a sucker for candids.

"People think I left Coldwater as quick as I could," she

says to the water, "and they're not wrong. But I came here first. I sat down right on the sand and stayed here till the sun went down. And every hour or so I'd ask, 'Am I doing the right thing?' Didn't know who I was asking. Didn't know if anyone was even listening. But I needed to make sure."

Gram leans forward until she's all but folded in half, resting her elbows on her thighs.

"It's easy, after almost thirty years, to make it sound like leaving was no big thing." She clears her throat until her voice sounds like it usually does, self-assured and dismissive. "I made my choice and acted on it. What's done is done. But I wasn't even thirty, leaving my family behind. And there was nowhere for me to go, either. My mama was gone. My sisters scattered who knows where. If I left, I was on my own. I'd never been that before—alone. There was my family, then Charlie, then the kids. How was I to know who I was without anyone else there to tell me?"

"But you figured it out," I say softly, camera abandoned in my lap.

"I did," she agrees, "and I didn't."

Gram straightens up and rolls her neck a few times. She runs a hand over her face. Then she turns fully to face me. "If you're gonna take my picture, I figured it ought to be somewhere important." She gestures to the water behind her. "And pretty."

"The change of scenery is nice," I agree.

I don't know if it's questions or comforts that sit on the tip of my tongue, but I know that Gram wouldn't appreciate either of them, not right now. So, I grab my camera, stand, and process things the way I do best.

◊

"One more!" I say, when we're both chilled from the water and hot from the sun.

It's been an hour and a half, and Gram's let me take picture after picture without (much) complaining. We're closer to the boardwalk now than we were before, and our photo session has mostly petered out, with me snapping the occasional picture between talking and seeing the sights until the roll is empty.

"Last one," Gram grumbles, eyeing me sidelong when I squish my face next to hers and take out my phone.

The sun is in our eyes and the ocean is in the background. Strawberry ice cream drips from my wrist and threatens to drip onto the screen. I smile wide. Gram barely smiles at all. It's only when we're on our way back to Coldwater with Gram already asleep beside me that I realize it's the first picture we've actually taken together.

◊

Gram goes to bed right after dinner, so Mom joins me on the porch to watch the sunset. It's something I do too inconsistently to be a habit, but there's something peaceful about watching the day end in pinks and golds.

"It's been a while," she says. I don't know if she means since we talked or since we watched the sunset together. Either way, I nod.

We're quiet as the sun turns everything gold. Finally, she says, "I miss you."

I'm here. She's here. We've both been here the whole summer. But I know what she means. The edges of our relationship are sharp and jagged now, easy to bump into and cut ourselves on.

"I miss you, too."

There's so much more to say.

There's nothing else to say.

The last bits of golden light linger down by the trunks of the trees. There are only a few minutes left until twilight.

THIRTY-FIVE

The house smells like cinnamon and syrup when I wake up. The TV is on a channel that alternates between color and static. The living room is filled with sunlight. The constantly running fan is off. And Gram is shivering under a bundle of blankets in her usual spot on the couch.

I say good morning and start to follow my nose to the kitchen before I pause.

"Gram? Are you okay?"

There's no grumbled, annoyed assurance. She only shivers harder, silent.

I go to her, placing a hand on her forehead and another to the side of her neck. Her heart races beneath my palm. Her skin is hot, so hot, and clammy. I try to take deep breaths through my quickly rising panic.

"What's wrong?" I ask her. "Can you hear me?"

She doesn't answer.

"Gram?"

Finally, she opens her eyes. I flinch. There's a haziness to them, like she's staring through smoke and finding it hard to place me. She squints, reaching a hand toward me. I take it in my own and squeeze.

"You changed your hair, Lacey," she murmurs through clenched teeth. I don't correct her, but my panic spikes. I try to think around the worry and the beating of my heart and the warmth of Gram's hand seeping into mine in the middle of this stifling, sunlit room.

There are steps I need to take. People I need to call. I try to remember.

1. I call Mom to tell her she needs to come home, now. I don't know if I explain anything, or do so coherently, but she tells me that she's in Delaware with Gloria, that she's on her way, that she'll be home as soon as she can.
2. Don't cry. Don't cry. Don't cry.
3. Call an ambulance. The operator is brusque and thick-accented. She tells me to stay with Gram. I tell her I haven't exactly made other plans for my morning.

The EMTs let me sit in the front. Kelli, the one driving, is saying something reassuring from the tone of her voice, but I'm not paying attention. I'm thinking about how the front of this ambulance reminds me of a moving van. How weird it is to be in one during the day, being whisked away to the hospital under a bright summer sun.

Death feels like it belongs to nighttime and rainy days, but it's barely ten thirty and the sun is blinding even when I shut my eyes.

And the panic is there, hovering like an echo over my shoulder. Winding its way around and around my body.

"The summer isn't over yet," I whisper.

"What's that, hon?" Kelli asks. I shake my head. She shoots me a slight smile and turns back to the road. "Nearly there."

◊

Sepsis. That's what the white-haired, white-coated doctor says. Something about infections and organ failure. Something about how it was good that I got her here so quickly. Something about the ICU and a ventilator.

"Is there an adult we can speak to?" a nurse asks.

She says it kindly. Her scrubs are a pleasant green to look at, like a lake or a dull jewel. They're the least muted thing I've seen at this hospital. I disappoint her when I shake my head no, say, "There's no one but me," because Mom is still on the road and Uncle Miles is always on the road. But she smiles anyway and tells me to ring the buzzer if either of us needs anything.

THIRTY-SIX

I drive myself crazy in the waiting room.

But it's better than staring at Gram, small and unconscious in her hospital bed. My camera is my only company, grabbed last minute on a stupid whim. I turn it over and over in my hands. Twisting every lens and knob and dial, running my hands over each curve and groove. I finger the film advance lever and meet resistance.

I'm out of film.

I'm out of film and I've barely finished taking all the photos I need to.

I try to think back. There was the full roll at the schoolhouse, the one I'm still waiting to get back from development, then another in Ocean City. This is a new roll, the last from Gram's box, but I've barely used it besides a test shot or two when I loaded it. There should be no way that I'm out already. Not unless she'd already used it.

My stomach drops.

There's no guarantee that just because this one's been used before the others were too. But if they were all together, it feels like a possibility. It makes sense to keep film waiting to be developed together, after all, separate from any new canisters.

The realization isn't much of one, but it's a shock anyway, amid all the other thoughts and emotions running through me.

Two thoughts take center stage.

The first is that I've probably ruined any pictures on that first roll.

The second is that Gram will want to see these when she wakes up.

She kept all the others for so long and they meant so much to her. If there are moments she captured that she hasn't seen in decades, I want to give them to her. I also want to get my other pictures back. I haven't heard from the shop since we dropped the film off days ago, and now it feels like a horrible sign.

I shift all my anxious energy into searching my camera bag for a receipt. I have so much trash in it for no reason—receipts from the diner and the ice cream shop; a crinkled, clear lollipop wrapper; even the newly broken cord of my phone charger. I set my camera aside and dump it all out, reading every scrap of paper repeatedly.

Finally, I find it. Snappy's Camera Shop—Laurel, Delaware.

I breathe a sigh of relief, snatching it up and dialing the number as quick as I can. The woman on the other end of the phone is polite as she informs me there were orders in before mine, that I'll need to give them a few more days.

"I don't know if I have that long," I blurt. Anxiety and

panic swirl in my gut as I try to remember to breathe. "Please," I beg. "I'll pay more money or something, but I need those photos tonight."

Sooner is better. I'll have the photos and they'll be ready and waiting for Gram to wake up.

There's a sigh on the other end. The rustling of paper. Finally, she speaks. "I can't do tonight," she says, firm enough that I bite down any response, "but I can have them ready for you before noon tomorrow."

Tomorrow.

It's not tonight, but it's the closest I can hope for.

I go back to Gram's room after I hang up, hoping for the company the waiting room lacks. It's a mistake. Gram is here but she's not *here*, ready and willing to talk movies or make snarky comments about the nurses. She's alive and breathing but so, so still compared to the restless energy filling me by the second.

I force myself to stay in my chair, if on the edge of it, constantly checking the analog clock on the wall and the time on my phone to compare the two, as if one might be faster than the other. I'm so anxious I nearly topple out of my chair when the door opens and Mom comes in.

"Jericka," she murmurs, already crossing the room to me and scooping me up before my name's all the way out of her mouth. "I'm so sorry, baby. I got here as fast as I could."

Her eyes flicker toward Gram. She breathes in slowly, holds me a little tighter. I want to hug her back, to be the comfort I know she needs, but I can't. I need to get out of here.

I really, really do.

"I'll be back soon, Mom, okay?" I say, slipping out of her grasp and over toward the door. "I just need some air." I meet her gaze. It's sad and worried and confused. I don't have time to try and figure out what's for me and what's for Gram. "You'll stay with her, right? You'll be right here?"

"I'll be right here," she promises.

I nod. Then I'm out of the room, speed walking down the hall and the three flights of stairs it takes to get to the main floor. I don't remember if Kat's working, but the relief I feel at the sight of her braided bun freezes me in place for half a breath.

I wait for her to finish helping the customer in front of me. When he's gone and she turns to me, her smile widens. Then it fades.

"You're not here for hot chocolate, I'm guessing," she says. And then, softer, "What's wrong?"

"Can you take me to Delaware tomorrow?" I should say hi or please or do you have to work tomorrow, but there's space for none of those words in my head, only a map with Laurel, Delaware, flashing red on it.

THIRTY-SEVEN

I'm making tea in the dark, in my pajamas, when Mom pads into the living room. She blinks at me when she turns on the light. Then sighs softly.

"Oh, Jericka."

I refocus on the cup of tea I've been trying to make for the past ten minutes. "I'm okay," I say automatically.

"Is that the answer you want to give?" she asks. I blink. It's something I haven't heard her say in years. She'd always ask me a question twice when I was upset, giving me the chance to tell the truth or to double down.

"I'm scared," I admit. "I don't know what happens when someone dies."

It sounds so silly. I know the gist. The funeral. The tears. The absence that everyone talks about. But I've never thought about it, really. I didn't know how much just waiting would hurt, like a timer in the pit of my stomach sending shock waves through me every few minutes.

"I don't know how anyone deals with it," I whisper, though I know that I'll have to. That every human being who has ever lived has felt this pain and survived it.

So why does it still feel like I'll be the first one who won't?

"No one else knows, either," Mom says, pulling me into a hug. "They just do it."

I take a deep breath. Then another. I take so many, one after the other, that it takes me a minute to realize I'm hyperventilating. All summer I've been fooling myself. I've been forming a relationship with the ghost of my grandmother, this person who isn't, and was never, going to live long enough to even be invited to graduation.

Mom rubs my back until breathing is easier and I burrow as close to her as I can get. One day, she'll die. And I will feel this pain again.

But she's here now: alive and warm and whole.

For now, I can put my hurt and anger aside.

For now, I can just take comfort in her presence.

◊

Kat and I are on the road bright and early. Mom's already left for the hospital and Uncle Miles is a state and a half away, scheduled for a noon arrival. I'm less panicked now. And there are snacks. Lukewarm hot chocolate and half a dozen doughnuts that Kat picked up on her way to my house.

I'm too tired to talk—sleep came in fitful starts and stops—so I watch Kat instead as she bites into a doughnut.

Jelly dribbles out the bottom and onto the steering wheel; she scoops it up with a finger and licks it off, grinning when she catches me watching.

"Wayne claims I pick the messiest foods to eat while I'm driving, just to show off."

"To show off your driving skills or your eating?"

She shrugs, eyes bright and teasing. "Whichever one you find more attractive."

I smile but don't say anything. I like the way Kat drives. Wild and fast, like she's eager to get wherever she's going, no matter where it is.

The morning light on the highway is gorgeous. It reflects the chrome of the cars and the guardrail and illuminates the wild grass on either side of the median. I'm wishing I had new film for my camera—or that my original hadn't gotten filled with enough sand, dirt, and water to kill the battery and damage the inside—every few minutes. My phone soothes the itch, but the results are lackluster.

"When'd you start taking pictures?" Kat asks suddenly. We've both been quiet for most of the drive, in between half-hearted attempts at I-spy and pointing out unfamiliar license plates.

"When I was eight, maybe?" I smile. "I got one of those little cheap Polaroids for Christmas, but I didn't really get the concept of film. I took pictures of everything I thought was interesting: ants in the kitchen, the blades of a ceiling fan, my mom's crossed legs where she sat on the couch."

I laugh. "My mom even got me a little photo album for

them. She said I had a good eye but maybe it was better suited for digital photography. She bought me a digital camera when I turned ten, but I got the one I brought here with me a few years ago, for my birthday. Uncle Miles pitched in."

"And that's what you want to do? In college and after? Take pictures?"

Yes and no. I don't want a studio where I take family portraits or those cute little newborn shoots. I want to travel and take pictures of the things that make me smile and the things I can't look away from. I want people to feel the same way I do when I look at something and think, *That's beautiful*. I think my photo project's helped make that clearer—I care more about the feelings my photos capture than what's in the pictures themselves. I don't really know what that means for a career.

For once, I don't think I care.

"I don't know," I say finally. "I'll keep taking pictures until I figure it out."

Kat smiles at me so warmly I feel my cheeks heat in response. "What about you?" I ask. "What do you want to be?"

She drums her fingers along the steering wheel in contemplation. Her nail polish is gone, I notice. "No clue. There's too much I like and nothing I'm good at. But I figure I've got the rest of my life to keep trying new things and figure it out."

It's such a Kat answer that it makes me smile.

For a moment, all of my swirling, rambling thoughts still. I breathe a little deeper. It must be audible because she glances my way.

"Almost there," she assures me.

I nod, leaning back in my seat, trying very hard not to think about how much it feels like I'm running away right now. I let myself sit with the thought until I can't keep it in and it fills up all the space in the car. I roll the window down as far as it can go.

Kat's quiet until we reach a stop sign, then she turns to fully face me. "You're allowed to run away sometimes."

I blink. "What?"

"If you only wanted to come pick up the film now because it gave you somewhere to run to . . . that's okay, you know."

I don't think so. But running from hard things is a family flaw, apparently.

"I'm not running," I promise her.

Promise myself.

◊

I don't open the folder of photos until we're parked in front of the hospital. I'm tempted to seal it back up again when I do.

Every picture is double exposed.

Every. Single. One.

I didn't realize that was a thing that could happen by accident, but it's staring me in the face now.

A picture of Gram on the couch layered over a shot of a close-up of the schoolhouse.

A dull yellow flower exposed over the shadows of the woods.

Mom covering up her childhood self, somehow midlaugh in both pictures, years and years apart.

There are more of them, so many more, and it makes my head spin to see the present literally layered on top of the past with barely any color separation.

Some are blurred in both timelines: blurry trees and a blurry sky on top of blurred kitchen tile.

But it's the last picture that makes me catch my breath. Layered over a poorly framed shot of Coldwater's welcome sign is an old-school selfie, angled from above and clearly on a self-timer. Gram is in the middle, shockingly young, with Mom and Uncle Miles cuddled up close. Their faces are scrunched in almost identical expressions, but Mom's eyes are closed.

"Are these . . . supposed to look like this?" Kat asks, leaning over the console for a better look.

I laugh. I can't help it; it's that or cry. "Definitely not."

"Well." She tilts her head to look at a picture of a bottle tree and the giant crab outside the diner. "It kinda works?"

I don't know if I'm opening my mouth to agree or disagree. It's better than a blank image, I guess, but I don't get the chance to do either. My phone buzzes in my lap and my heart leaps into my throat. It's Mom.

ETA?

Here.

I carefully put all the photos back in their sleeve and stare straight ahead at the small building in front of us.

"I still owe you five dollars," I murmur.

"What?"

"For my drinks that first day." I don't know why I bring it

up, except that I've made so many memories in this tiny hospital that I'm too afraid to go into now.

She snorts. "It was your welcome gift."

"It was a pretty good one."

She laughs. "Oh, yeah. Hot drinks in the summer. Perfect gift."

"What's a good goodbye gift, do you think?"

"Depends on why you're saying goodbye."

I turn to look at her. She's a little blurry through the sheen of tears I try to blink away. Her eyes dart back and forth between mine, and the smile she gives me is soft when I ask, "What should I get you, before we're both out of here?"

Kat presses a kiss to my cheek. "Maybe ask me again when we're closer to leaving."

THIRTY-EIGHT

Mom and Uncle Miles are talking quietly in the hall when I get off the elevator, and I know she's gone before either of them looks at me. I know that I've missed it. Missed her. It's something in the air, the smell of rain before a downpour hits.

Gram is dead.

"That was quick," I say.

My voice trembles. So does the envelope of pictures in my hand; pictures I won't get to show Gram after all. Mom is a step ahead of me, as always. She wraps me into a hug just as the first few tears start to fall.

There's an impression of our moms that we have that starts from birth and only grows from childhood: that they can make everything better.

It doesn't work this time.

She doesn't say anything. No reassurances, no apologies.

She just holds me, the two of us swaying as she rocks us back and forth in a hospital hallway. Her chin rests against the top of my head, the side of my face squished into her chest. I can hear her heart pounding.

THIRTY-NINE

Things that I should have told my grandmother: a random list.

- Once, someone dared me to eat a worm when I was in third grade. I ate half of it, collected my five dollars, then threw up behind a tree when no one was looking.
- When I was six, I hid Mom's car keys in my dollhouse before she left for work because I didn't want to go to school and I didn't want her to leave.
- I'm afraid of jellyfish.
- I like syrup on pancakes but not on waffles.
- I didn't lose my first tooth until I was almost eight, and it got stuck in a pear, so I threw it out.
- The first time I had a panic attack was in the principal's office in elementary school

because I thought I was in trouble. Turns out, Mom was just picking me up early.

- Sometimes, when I could hear Mom crying in the middle of the night, I'd turn on my TV so she'd have to come in my room to tell me to turn it off.
- Once, I tried to bring home a chipmunk I found in the bushes outside of our condo.
- I don't actually think *In the Heat of the Night* is Sidney Poitier's best movie.
- Before I met you, I thought you were the worst woman in the world. I thought Mom was stupid for coming back and dragging me with her. I didn't think you deserved a second chance.
- You should say sorry to the people you hurt.
- I know you were trying to make things up to Mom through me. I forgive you. But you should have tried harder to make things up to her and Uncle Miles, too.
- You were worth giving a second chance.
- I wish I could have shown you those pictures.
- I love you.
- Mom keeps a long red coat in the back of our downstairs closet that she's never worn, and I think it used to be yours.

FORTY

I sleep a lot, the day after. I cry some. Most of the day feels the same from one moment to the next: none of the extremes I expected. None of the much-discussed stages of grief.

Instead, it feels like I could stare at a blank wall for days. Or I could scream.

And none of it would matter. And all of it would feel the same.

I find myself flipping through the pictures every hour like something about them will have changed.

By the fifth time or so, I've almost memorized every beauty mark on Gram's face. By the tenth, I finally spot an echo in the background of one of them.

It's faint, and could just as easily be a smudge of light from the developing process as anything else, but it's not. I *know* it's not. The shape is too human, the aura warping the trees closest to it like it's been photoshopped. And where most of the photo is the brown of old film poorly color corrected, there's something luminous about the echo.

It could just be more double exposure.

But it isn't.

I flip through the others, but I don't find any more. I reach for my phone on the nightstand and then sit up quickly, remembering the memory card from my camera. Maybe I caught something similar. The camera might be broken, but I never actually looked at the pictures stored in its memory, I realize. I'd been so caught up in the physical body being broken, then getting the SLR from Gram, and everything else that's been going on since the river party that the memory card slipped my mind completely.

But the card isn't on my nightstand, even though that's the last place I remember putting it.

It's not in my camera bag or in my suitcase or in any of my dresser drawers.

My frustration builds, and so does the pressure behind my eyes. The memory card isn't a big deal, I try to reassure myself, but it's a lie. There are pictures of Gram on it, potentially pictures of echoes, and all the other pictures I'd taken in Coldwater before my camera broke. If it's lost . . .

I swallow back tears and crawl halfway under the bed. There are more cobwebs and dead flies than I know what to do with, but, thankfully, my memory card is there, too. Black and dull against the dark wood.

I snatch it up and I'm back on my bed in an instant,

booting up my laptop. For a moment, anticipation is all I feel. It's a bright jitteriness that overshadows grief. A nice change of pace.

As usual when I'm in a hurry, my laptop is slow. It restarts itself before I can type in my password and takes its sweet time coming back on. Nearly ten minutes pass from the time I open my laptop to when I can finally stick the memory card in. The pictures, at least, boot up quickly. In the folder, I catch glimpses of Kat, of Mom, of Coldwater as I was first introduced to it.

I catch glimpses of Gram.

I move the mouse to click on a picture of her first. But my mouse is slow. Or my computer hates me. Or the universe is cruel and amused. Because as I go to click, a small window pops up. And instead of clicking on Gram, or even the option to save the photos on the card to my laptop, I click on format.

Format, meaning erasing the card's memory.

And the folder of pictures disappears in an instant, like a magic trick.

All I can do is stare.

And when I'm done staring, I click on every folder I can open. I restart the laptop. I google. But Google is clear: Besides scam recovery software and software that costs hundreds of dollars just for the *possibility* of getting the pictures back, there's no solution. The pictures are as gone as Gram is.

Laughter builds in me so quickly that it bursts out in a loud rush. I fall forward with the force of it, giggling and gasping for breath, trying to bury my face in a pillow to muffle the sound.

It helps when the laughter turns into sobs.

FORTY-ONE

I drag myself out of my room the second day to help Mom go through Gram's things. She doesn't have a lot, and what she does have is mostly sentimental. Old drawings and baby clothes yellowed from age. Ticket stubs and crumpled, handwritten notes and postcards written and stamped but unaddressed. We separate her whole life into piles labeled TRASH and KEEP.

When we're done, Mom pours us both sweet tea. It's the last pitcher Gram made, I notice, and we escape the heat of the house for the heat of outside. The bags under Mom's eyes are more noticeable in the sun. Her hair is hidden beneath a scarf, and there's something black and smudged on her cheek. I want to ask her if she's okay, even though I know that's a stupid question.

How are you, Mom, now that Gram is gone, like dead, not just gone like left?

I must stare at her too hard for too long because she offers me a small smile.

"I'm tired," she says, answering my unasked question. "You know, I almost expected her to be one of them." She gestures toward the yard, empty of echoes for now, with her glass. "Roaming. Stuck here."

I don't know if it's wistfulness or sadness in Mom's voice.

She finishes the last of her tea in a few long swallows and stands. "Probably for the best," she says. "I think she would've driven the other ghosts mad. You coming inside?"

"In a minute." It's nowhere close to sunset, but I want to enjoy the view from this porch while I still can.

I don't know how long I sit there before they come. The sky doesn't do anything drastic, so it can't be too long. But one moment it's me and the crickets and the fluffy tail of a stray sticking out from under the crawl space. The next there's a handful of echoes in front of me.

I should go inside.

I should go inside and lock the door and save myself a headache. Or a crying fit.

But I don't.

My hands tighten around my cup, but I don't move. Neither do they. We stare at each other, me and these shadows of the past, and I feel . . . the same.

It takes me a second. Then I mirror the sad smile the echo closest to me wears. "This is it, huh? How you guys always feel?"

This: lingering, low-grade grief.

This: deep, unanswerable quiet.

This: knowledge that there is nothing you can do to make things okay, if okay is a thing that exists at all.

They don't answer me. Of course they don't.

Now would be a good time to photograph them. I got a fresh roll of film from the camera shop in Laurel—there's nothing stopping me from filling it with shots of the ghostly women in my front yard. But this feels different from every other time I've seen them. They're not wandering now, keeping an eye on the town or tracing old routes. They're here deliberately. For Gram? For me?

I feel like a different Jericka from the one who entered the schoolhouse, or even the one who came out of it. She'd known loss—the loss of homes and schools and friends—but she was inexperienced with grief. The way it scoops away a piece of you. The way it changes your own memories, so even the bad feels nostalgia-tinged. I didn't lose everything when I lost Gram, though I lost enough. The echoes lost everything—including themselves.

When I came to Coldwater, the echoes were a story, then a fascination, then a project. They were a point of uniqueness that added to the town's history, a contentious point among some of its residents and my family. But I don't think there was a point when I ever actually remembered that they were just people.

People who had wanted a better future for a growing town, people with families and dreams and futures themselves.

We're more alike than I gave either of us credit for, I realize. The echoes might be stuck in their grief strongly enough that it feels like it's who they are, but I've been stuck, too. I've been so focused on everything I've lost or so fixated on everything that's to come that I've barely paid attention to what's here: the friends and family I do have, the space that my present self exists in.

It's been exhausting trying to live in the past, the present, and the future all at once. It must be even more so to be a near-physical embodiment of grief and memory.

The difference, though, is that I can change. I already have. At least, I hope so.

I'm not sure the dead get the same luxury.

Not even echoes.

Stay.

It's quiet. Less insistent than it normally is. I don't know what it means. Maybe it's a plea. Maybe it's just a fact. They have to stay in the past; they have no choice.

Or maybe it's a comfort, after all this time, to be present to see what Coldwater and its people have become since they were alive.

"I can stay for a little while," I say. "But not forever."

They don't respond. Of course they don't.

Eventually, the echoes drift away in silence and I stay on the porch. I watch the kitten under the crawl space dart out toward a huddle of birds and watch as they escape in a flutter of gray-brown wings.

◊

I spend the week leading up to Gram's homegoing celebration convincing people to let me take their picture in their favorite place in town. Kat comes with me. She's good with the older people, at convincing them I'm trustworthy, or that she is. The ones our age don't need convincing.

In four days, I find more new places in Coldwater than I have in the past couple months. I sit in the middle of cornfields until all I can see is sky and cornstalks. I kneel in the dirt in a u-pick strawberry farm. I even trek up and down the row of graveyards in the Zion United Methodist Church's overgrown cemetery, doing my best not to step on sunken headstones.

Uncle Miles and I are on our way to the American Legion now, bright and early. I'm so anxious that the prints keep spilling from the envelope onto the floor of Uncle Miles's car. I want to create my mini gallery before everyone arrives.

It takes two rolls of double-sided tape and a few poster boards, but I feel good when it's finished. I've organized the photos into a map as best I could: a layout of Coldwater via people's favorite places.

Whenever Mom and I stayed somewhere long enough, I made a list of my top three favorite places. They were never very important. A movie theater I'd gone to with a new group of friends. A park I walked past after school. The pond behind a group of condos. But I told myself that if I could narrow it down to just one, I'd consider that place home.

I've come close.

Two. One and a half.

But I've never been as certain as the people who let me take their portraits were. Taking the pictures was harder than I expected, mostly because people are used to smiling and waiting. But people relax in their favorite spaces. All it took was me staying quiet long enough to help them forget I was there.

Looking at the portraits now, it seems to have worked. People's nerves shine through. Their awkwardness and wariness and excitement. Few of them are looking at me. And my camera's not really focused on them, either. It's focused on everything else. On the shimmering river in the background or the paneling of a house, the silky fibers of rows and rows of corn or the curved metal of a bench.

The focus is on Coldwater. The people are just at the center of it.

In the middle, where the bottle tree would be in this crude photo-focused map, I've put my double-exposed pictures. Strange past layered on top of strange future. The dichotomy of a town.

It's not exactly Magnum Gallery in Paris. But it works. And it's the only photo project I'm determined to think about right now. At the end of the day, all photography is, really, is an attempt at keeping something, or someone, alive forever. This is mine.

All morning, people come in and out of the American Legion. They bring food and tell us how sorry they are before congregating in corners to gossip. Mom and Uncle Miles get folded into hugs by old people who treat them like little kids.

I get lost in the shuffle, not quite as well-known or at the forefront of people's minds as they are. I don't mind.

I grab a plate of food for myself and settle into a chair in a corner of the room, watching people look at my pictures, pointing out themselves or people they know.

"Jelly Bean."

I'd recognize Cora's voice even if she hadn't used her nickname for me. When I stand to greet her, she pulls me into a crushing hug. It lasts just long enough for me to relax before she pulls back to look at me.

"How're you doing, honey?"

No one has asked me that yet. Mom and Uncle Miles have asked if I'm okay a few times, but that's not a question anyone ever wants to say no to. Kat's asked me what I need, but I feel selfish answering that, after everything she's done for me. *How are you doing* is so much more open-ended.

I don't know where to start. So, I tell her the truth. "I'm getting used to it."

I'm getting used to the absence. To the grief. To this new state of self that is apparently the aftermath of death.

Cora nods. The look she gives me is so sympathetic it makes me want to cry. I look away from her quickly, scanning the room. "Where's my dad?"

She nods toward the food tables, where he stands, to my surprise, next to Mom. His hand is on her shoulder as he says something to her, and Mom turns to bury her face into his chest. As her shoulders shake, he switches to rubbing small circles on her back.

I glance at Cora, but she only smiles. "Your mama needs comforting right now. And she's known your dad her whole life. He loves her. He should be here for her."

"But aren't you . . ." *Jealous* feels like the wrong word. "Uncomfortable?"

She laughs softly, smoothing down my hair to press a kiss to the top of my head. "Love doesn't make me uncomfortable, Jericka. It comforts me."

I glance back at my parents. There's love between them. It's in the curve of Mom's cheek pressed to his chest and in the surety of Dad's hands on her back. It's not the same love he shares in smiles with Cora across the dining room table or even the love they might have shared before they had me, but it's love all the same. And Cora's right—it's comforting to see.

◊

Mom finds me later, still in the corner, eating a slice of sweet potato pie. She gives me a squeeze before pulling up a chair. "Feeling okay?"

I mumble something reassuring around a mouthful of pie. Her lips quirk into a half smile before she sighs. "It's been a long day. But we need to say something before we can end this thing."

Panic is quick to surface and quicker to consume me. "Something like what? In front of everyone?"

"It's just a few words to remember her by."

I turn to look at her. "Do you want to do that?" I can't

imagine that any of the good memories she has with Gram are ones that she wants to share. She hasn't even shared them with me.

She avoids the question. "It's tradition at these things." Mom kisses my cheek. "Five minutes, okay? Don't overthink it. Just say whatever comes to mind."

I watch her as she walks away, slipping so easily back into a crowd eager to get her attention. I turn back to my pie, but my appetite is gone. I'm supposed to share my memories of Gram with all these people who knew her for so much longer than I did, or who thought they knew her, and for what? To ease everyone's grief? To paint some picture of her that makes her worthy of their grief at all?

What would I share, anyway? What is two months' worth of memories in the grand scheme of things?

My chest constricts. I take shallow breaths to breathe around the panic, but I can't get enough air. It leaves my lungs quicker than I can replenish it. I grip the sides of my chair to ground myself. I don't want to make a scene. I don't want to draw attention to myself. I just want to breathe.

"Hey." Kat's voice is soft and suddenly right next to me. The weight of her hand is on my shoulder. I didn't know she was here. It's unlike her not to make her presence known. It's unlike me not to have noticed her. "You okay?"

I nod. Because even as my panic attack kicks into full gear, I don't want to worry her. I don't want her going to get Mom or trying to calm me down herself. I feel like I'm constantly breaking down around Kat.

But apparently, she can read my mind. She's kneeling in front of me before I can wave her away, bracing herself with both hands on my knees. "Talk to me, Jericka. What do you need?"

I need to breathe.

I need to cry.

I need, I need, I need.

Finally, I manage to whisper, "I need air."

FORTY-TWO

Kat pulls me outside.

I let her guide me away from the building as I take deep breath after deep breath. I focus on the weight of her palm, the rise and fall of my chest. I focus on the wind and the feel of it against my face, the flags flapping lazily overhead. By the time we stop walking, I'm calmer and we're standing in front of the bottle tree in the middle of town.

Colored glass absorbs the sunlight. The bottles knock into one another like wind chimes, carrying the soft tinkling into open air.

I turn to Kat. "Why are we here?"

She's not looking at me or the tree. Instead, she's riffling through a bigger bag than I've ever seen her carry. With a huff, she kneels and dumps everything out instead. There's twine and tape and a thick, black marker. And there are glass bottles. Four of them, scattered in the grass.

"I didn't know which color you'd want," she explains.

"So, I brought options. The tree's not just for warding off bad spirits. It helps us remember, too."

She reaches for the marker. "We mark up the bottles meant for remembering." She points and I follow her finger. A branch on my left is weighed down by dozens of bottles, and each of them bear writing too small to see from here. "The people we're remembering don't always have to be dead, either. Me and Wayne put one up for our mom a while back."

"How's the bottle supposed to help?"

She smiles. "You whisper your favorite memories of the person into it and the bottle keeps them here. Holds them even if you forget."

I run a hand over the bottle closest to me. It's clear, like an old milk bottle. There's an aging green one, an amber one the color of a medicine bottle, and one a deep, almost royal, blue. I study them, trying to figure out which one is best suited to Gram. I didn't know her favorite color. It's such an inconsequential thing to know about another person, but right now it feels huge. It feels like everything is riding on something simple that I don't know and will never get the chance to. Panic builds inside of me again. Rising from my gut and swimming in my rib cage and filling my lungs . . .

"Hey." Kat interrupts my spiraling thoughts. She's a blur surrounded by sunlight and colored glass. She squeezes my hand and I blink away tears. "You're okay."

I'm not, but it's a little easier to breathe with her hand in mine. I inhale deeply, past panic. I reach for the nearest bottle. The green one.

I start to whisper into it. Even as I speak, I don't remember half of what I say. It's all a ramble of remembrance: the way she smelled, the way she'd dig her nails into the armrest during chemo, the way she laughed during her favorite scene in *Carmen Jones*, the snort she'd give when she was annoyed by something but not enough to comment on it. By the time I'm done I'm crying and the bottle feels, strangely, ridiculously, heavier in my grip.

"Ready?" she asks. I nod. I'm as ready as I can be.

The nearest branch is still a few feet taller than I am until Kat hoists me up. I try not to wobble, tying the twine around the branch as quickly and tightly as I can. I'm scared the bottle will break. Scared that I'll lose my memories of Gram.

When she sets me down, though, the twine holds. Gram's bottle—with her name and the date of her death barely visible in thick black strokes on the bottom—joins the others.

◊

I'm not prepared for this, I think as I face half the town, every one of their faces expectant as they stare back.

I know some of them didn't like Gram. I know most of them probably judged her. I don't know how many of them are here out of genuine mourning or just nosiness.

"I was going to come up here and say sweet things about Gram. The thing is, though," I say, "I think everyone here has talked about her enough. So many of you put so much focus on her leaving, and for what? To make yourselves feel better? To forget that maybe you wanted to leave, too?" I'm not sure this is what Mom had in mind when she asked me to say something, but it's too late now. I ignore the murmurs that start up. "She told me something once. She said that when she lived here, it was only the ghosts that reminded her that she was somebody. Only the dead made her feel like she belonged."

More murmurs. Whispers. Louder now. I try to tune them out.

"I didn't know my grandmother for most of her life. Not even for most of mine. I don't know what type of person she was when she lived here—if she was rude or loud or skipped church a little too often. But I know that she was just as deserving of love and belonging as any of us. That she deserves to be remembered for who she was, not just a choice she made thirty years ago."

I scan the room. There are so many people I don't know and even more that I only half recognize. I wonder how many of them can see and feel the echoes.

"The same goes for the ghosts and the schoolhouse."

I take a deep breath. I know I'm rambling, but, for once, I don't care. When else will I get to talk to so much of the town at once? When else will I get a chance to try and help the dead women who, if not helped me, have at least made things in my life a little more interesting?

"I don't know what any of you can or can't see or feel. I don't know what you believe in. But I know Coldwater is a place with a long memory. You wouldn't have your thirty-year-old rumors if it wasn't. So, imagine there was a fire here, right now, and we all died. Just like that. No warning. No escape. Now imagine if everyone chose to forget. Our names, our faces, what we'd done. What if all that was left of us were the ruins of this building that everyone passed by but no one gave a second thought to. How would that make you feel? How *does* it make you feel?"

I expect whispers or annoyed sighs, even laughter. I'm talking about ghosts, after all.

What I don't expect is the silence.

It's not light—there's weight to it. Tension, maybe even irritation. But I'd like to think there's thoughtfulness, too.

I clear my throat. "I know how it makes me feel. This town was my first home and it's the first place that's *felt* like home in a long time, maybe ever." My eyes find Mom's in the front row. "I understand why people want to leave. I understand why they want to stay, too. There's history here—it says so right on the welcome sign. It's a sad one. But it didn't start that way. And that's not all it is. Coldwater started as a place of hope and love and connection. It was a safe haven for people who'd had little safety in the world.

"I'm not asking for trouble, or trying to stick my nose where some of you might not think it belongs. I'm just saying that maybe the first step to getting people to stay here, to getting them to come back, is remembering what type of place Coldwater was to begin with. Who built this town and why that legacy is so important." I gesture to my makeshift gallery wall. "That's the thing about memory. You have to take the bad with the good. It can be painful, but it can also show us who we are and where we come from."

I glance down at the picture I took off the wall. It's the schoolhouse, burned and abandoned and ruined. Sunspots surround it. Underneath is a field of flowers, faded with age and color correction. Kids I can't make out lying in the middle of them.

"When I got here, the sign that welcomed me told me that this is a place that restores and cherishes its history." I lift my head. Everyone's eyes are still on me. I don't look away. "I haven't seen that. The history is here, all right, but it's not restored. It's not cherished. And it's not up to me to tell you, any of you, to do it. But I think we should and I think it should start with the schoolhouse. Maybe that will make Coldwater feel less like a monument to the past and a little more like home."

◊

Mom's waiting for me at the bottom of the small stage when I step down. I'm in her arms before I can even pretend to protest. "I think you scandalized everyone with your ghost talk," she murmurs into my hair.

"I guess I should expect to be part of the gossip for the next few decades, then," I say, and she laughs.

She catches one of my stray tears with her fingers when she lets me go, studying my face closely. "Did I ever show you my favorite place?" she asks finally.

I wipe the rest away myself. "I didn't know you had one."

She smiles. It's not a sad smile or the tired smile that's been her default lately. "I have a favorite place everywhere I go," she says, surprising me. "This one just happens to be the original."

◊

"It had to be close by," Mom says as we slip into the woods behind Gram's house, "in case Miles needed me or my dad was in a mood. But it was quiet and cool in the summers, and it reminded me of my mama."

It's early evening and still bright out, but barely any light penetrates here. The woods are denser than they are by the river, the trees pressed tight together. They feel more protective than anything. Like we've stepped somewhere the outside world can't reach us. Like if I cry or scream the trees might brush against me and the birds might sing wordless comfort.

"Why'd it remind you of Gram?"

Mom's quiet. We walk until we come across a pond. It's small, little more than a puddle, half-covered in green algae, but the sight of it is peaceful.

Finally, she says, "We used to come here sometimes. Just the two of us. My dad would be gone and Miles would be napping or with a neighbor and we'd just . . . sit." She sits now, brushing dirt and leaves off the top of a rotting log. "She called it our time away."

Mom's facing me, but her eyes are distant. "Maybe she

saw her own restlessness in me. Or maybe she just wanted to give me a little bit of time to get out of that house."

I don't think I've seen Mom cry. Not since Gram died. But tears pool in her eyes now, glittering like the pond. She doesn't bother blinking them away.

"I'm pretty sure I talked her ear off. Sometimes she'd bring her camera and take pictures or she'd bring a book, but she'd still just let me talk. I didn't get to do a lot of that normally. My dad liked it quiet."

I try to picture my mom, the little girl in the pictures, moving and breathing and talking. I try to hear her voice, but all I hear is her voice as it is now. "What did you talk about?"

She shrugs. "I couldn't tell you. It was just the time spent that I remember. The image of her sitting next to me and listening. I think that's probably what I hated her the most for: all the memories I have. For letting them fill the space she left behind. Because I know that she loved us, and I'd seen how happy she could be. Hidden in these trees, Jericka, she was . . ."

Mom breaks off with a soft laugh and shakes her head. "She was so alive. So full of whatever it is that people usually keep to themselves. And she shared it with me here. And that just made everything a little harder to deal with, after. And now."

Little by little, her voice goes quiet. Little by little, my mom curls into herself. She sits so still that it's hard to pinpoint when she starts to cry in earnest.

I don't think now is one of the times when companionable

silence works best, so I hug her. I put everything into that hug. My entire life. This entire summer. My hurt and my anger. My sadness and my love. We both hold on tight.

Hugging Mom now, in this place she shared with Gram, feels like home. Like how I always wanted Jersey to feel. Like how I quietly hoped Coldwater would.

Far from perfect, but still good. Still a comfort.

"I want to stay," I murmur into my mom's shoulder.

FORTY-THREE

Turns out, there are some issues with that. One being that Mom and Uncle Miles are selling the house. But not immediately because it needs some work. Construction, reconstruction, repair. Whatever it is, none of it's suitable to a person still living there.

The main issue, though, is that Mom refuses to let me stay here alone.

She does what she can to talk me out of it. She reminds me of the weeks left before school starts, weeks better spent with Leslie or at the beach. Weeks that we could use to go on a vacation or that I could use to prepare for senior year and college applications and all the life left to be lived outside of Coldwater.

But if there's anything I got from Mom, it's her stubbornness. So, I don't relent.

I want to be here without the fear that Gram is going to die at any moment or that Mom is going to whisk us away again. I want to eat dinner with Dad and his family—*my* family. I want to go dorm shopping with Kat. I want to see Uncle Miles's house for myself in a rare moment of stillness for him.

And I want to watch the echoes. From afar, from up close. To form a new understanding of who they are and, yes, to see if they can ever photograph well, if at all. I want to help with the renovations at the schoolhouse, too. There's nothing happening—not yet, not officially. But word around town is that there'll be a bake sale fundraiser next month.

Mom listens to me. And she doesn't agree. But we do come to a compromise.

Cora and Dad are waiting by the front door when we pull up. I can see Marcus's and Kya's faces peeking out from behind the curtains at the window; Kya ducks when I spot her, but Marcus only grins and sticks his tongue out at me.

Mom's fingers flex around the steering wheel as she parks. For a minute, we just sit there. Then she sniffs and rubs her nose, laughing when I turn to look at her. "This was hard enough the first time," she says in that soft, croaky voice that precedes tears.

"It's only a couple of weeks, Mom."

She nods, but her eyes study me like it will be forever. I wonder what she's thinking. Reliving. So, I ask her. There's a lot I probably still don't know, and plenty I probably never will, but I can at least start asking.

She places a hand on my cheek and smiles. Her fingertips are cold. "It feels like I'm always leaving you when we're here," she says.

"You're not leaving me. I want to stay."

Mom nods. "I know."

Her hand falls away from my face to squeeze my shoulder. She studies me like I'm something she's trying very hard to memorize—or like I'm a memory in need of updating.

Our goodbye is brief. We've already said our real goodbye in the woods behind the house the day of Gram's homegoing. But I squeeze her now, giving love first instead of just returning it, wrapping her in all the love I wish I could have given the little girl who stood dry-eyed and confused in the parking lot of her school.

Some part of me finally relaxes.

Everything between us is not settled. There's an ache in my chest that will probably always be there and that will hurt some days more than others. We'll definitely never get back to what we were.

But we have time. We'll form something new.

After one last squeeze, I get out of our car and head over to Dad and Cora. I wave and wave until Mom's license plate is unreadable, from distance, from dust. When there's nothing left to see, I turn to Dad and Cora, who are watching me with matching expressions, though I can't make out how they're feeling or what it means. Kat's car pulls up, easing some of my anxiety.

"I'll be back in time for dinner," I promise.

"Go on," Dad says. "The door'll be unlocked."

I go, sliding into the passenger side of Kat's car, and we're off, down an empty road that's become so familiar even its potholes aren't a surprise. It's ages before we reach a traffic light. When the sound of tires on asphalt fades and between the hum of the engine and the music on the radio, I hear another car.

It's an edge-of-the-ear sound. Not really a sound at all, but I turn toward the road anyway. There are no other cars besides Kat's. No one's zooming past or heading toward us. No one real, anyway. But there's a shadow of a car next to ours, wispy, flickering like it's made of smoke. Indistinguishable by color or brand. An *echo* of a car.

The woman in it looks a little more substantial, but just barely. She looks how she does in pictures. Young and determined; a little angry and a little excited. Her hair curls around her head like a halo, and as I watch, she flexes her fingers on the wheel. Fear twists her expression. She turns all the way around to stare at the road back toward town. And then she faces forward. Her expression fades back into determination and she's gone.

Straight ahead. Out of Coldwater.

I turn to Kat, but she's already looking at me. A soft smile plays on her lips. I want to ask if she saw what I did, but I don't need to know whether it was real or not. Instead, I return her smile. She's leaving soon, too. Off to Virginia. But for now, she's right here beside me.

"Do you think we can just drive for a bit?" I ask.

Kat doesn't ask where. She doesn't ask for how long. "Do you want me to go straight or do you want me to turn around?"

The sun is shining directly into the car, the hard yellow of noon, but both our visors stay up. The vents do their best to crank out cold air, but it's getting warmer and warmer inside.

I lean forward to kiss her, just because I can. Her lips still taste like strawberries. Then I relax into the passenger seat and shut my eyes. "Surprise me?"

Kat rolls the windows down and pulls off. I let myself stay adrift in the car's movement, almost weightless with how fast she drives. I don't know how far we'll go or what will happen next. I just know that I'm moving forward with wind in my hair and the cloyingly sweet smell of bubble gum in my nose.

ACKNOWLEDGMENTS

This book wasn't written in the void (most of it, anyway) which means there are many, many people to thank. So many, in fact, that I've broken them down into categories.

FAMILY:

This would be endless if I named every single person related to me, but I do love you all so much! I couldn't have asked for a better family on either side, siblings, aunts, uncles, cousins, grandparents, all of y'all. Please don't text me asking if any of these characters are you. They're not. Don't worry about it.

FRIENDS (REAL LIFE, DISCORD, PEOPLE WHO DON'T KNOW I EXIST, ETC.):

Big thank-you to Alex, Julie, Molly, Cynthia, Kayla (yes, you've graduated from sister to friend), Sabrina, Bianca, Natalie, Anna, McKenna, Katherine, Brittany 1, Brittany 2, Sean, Lauren, Angela, Anna, Eleanor, Gabby, Harriet, Liz, Christy, Alison, Gareth,

Yukari, my NaNoWriMo pen pals, the casts of both *Dimension20* and *Critical Role*, and other people I'm sure I'm accidentally forgetting, for any number of things, including but not limited to: listening to me complain, doing fun things with me, being generally hilarious and/or lovely, inspiring me creatively, gossiping with me, jumpstarting my hyperfixations, and being nice to me in any way at all.

EMERSON FRIENDS:

There are actually a lot of you, which is forever a shock to me! Enormous thank-yous to Madeline, Nihal, Prerna, Christina, Dave, Winelle, and Porsha, for being my classroom buddies, my whining-about-our-theses buddies, and more. Your general belief in and hype for my writing, especially when I wasn't feeling it myself, meant the world. You all are some of my favorite readers and hype men and I can't wait to return the favor as soon as possible. This is the last bit of sappiness you guys will ever get from me, so savor this.

EMERSON PROFESSIONALS:

I have to thank Emerson College as a whole to begin with here. The fellowship I received, the professors I learned from, the friends I made there have all contributed so positively to my life that I am a different person now than I might have been otherwise. Thank you to Jabari Asim for being such a brilliant, insightful person and writer who has been in my corner since before day one and straight through to the end (and beyond). Thank you to Steve Yarborough for being a lovely first introduction to workshops and for being my thesis reader. Thank you to Kim McLarin, who allowed me to switch into her already full novel workshop class, and who, without her candor and knowledge, this book would be a bit of a mess. Thank you to Julie Glass, who made workshops a delight. Thank you to Pam Painter, who helped me hone my craft through flash fiction. And thank you to Mako Yoshikawa, who really knows how to build a girl's self-esteem (and whose tree is the stuff of legends and stories).

PUBLISHING PEEPS:

Most people don't know how books go from words on a screen to actual books that you hold in your hand (or that you read on another screen or listen to), but it's a lot of work and there are a lot of amazing, hardworking people doing it! Thank you to Patrice Caldwell for making me feel like this little story of mine was something special and worth representing, and for your support along the way. Thank you to Trinica Sampson-Vera for your kindness, amazing email response time, and generally being so on top of things that it's wild.

Thank you to Elizabeth Lee for taking a chance on me and Jericka and acquiring this book and for your love of it when it was still very half-baked. Thank you to Grace Kendall and Asia Harden for taking up the mantle and being the best editors I could've asked for for a story that means so much to me. The two of you and your kindness, understanding, and praise made working on something so emotional worth it when things got rough. Thank you to L. Whitt for such a stunner of a cover and to Ilana Worrell and Celeste Cass for turning my atrocious grammar into something readable and book-shaped.

Thank you also to Pouya Shahbazian, Katherine Curtis, Tracy Williams, and the entire New Leaf team.

MOM:

Oh, Mom. There's so much to say here that I could write a whole other book! I'm not, that would take years, so let me just say this: Every iteration of you is the best mother I could have asked for and I would not be me if I didn't have you.

Your voice is a lovely one to have in my head. And, you know, on the other end of the phone all the time.

ME:

I started working on this book after an incredibly long year full of change. My grandmother had died and I'd graduated from college and started grad school in a new city and state I'd only visited once before. I had no clue what I wanted to do next . . . except write.

So, I did. Writing this book was one of the hardest things I've had to do but it was also one of the best decisions I've ever made and I couldn't be prouder of myself for doing it.

YOU:

In my mind, *Something Kindred* is first and foremost a journal of sorts, a love letter to the women in my life second, and my MFA thesis third. To think that you, reader, have come to the end of what is now a book and are reading these acknowledgments is strange to consider, even as I write this. But I very much appreciate it. Jericka would, too.

I hope this book was what you needed or, perhaps, that it will be.

Thank you so much for reading.